"You have a lot of nerve coming back after twelve years and trying to pick up like nothing ever happened after you left."

Alicia closed her eyes, inhaled deeply. "I get it. You're a naval officer who probably has a gal in every port. Well, Lieutenant Sloan, my little part of the world doesn't have a dock. It's centered around a four-year-old child. I'm her whole world. And I don't take risks with it."

"I get it."

"No, I don't think you do. I have responsibilities to Lauren and have no intention of jeopardizing that by dating. Let alone having sex in a ____d-up field with a man I haven't seen or h____ ____ n over a decade."

"Don't worry ab____ ____k."

"I don't want y____

"Never." He'd n____ ____ also never stop wanting her wit____ ____ or his being. *Never.*

NAVY SEAL SURRENDER

Angi Morgan

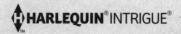

Recycling programs for this product may not exist in your area.

Many moons ago, I graduated high school with a small group of kids. Brian & Johnny are fictional characters but named after two men who won't be returning at our next reunion. Several of the names in the Sloane brothers' stories are familiar to my friends, but do not reflect any of their true personalities. All the characters are fictional, but not my friendship with my classmates.

ISBN-13: 978-0-373-74816-7

NAVY SEAL SURRENDER

Printed in U.S.A.

HARLEQUIN®

www.Harlequin.com

ABOUT THE AUTHOR

Angi Morgan writes Harlequin Intrigue novels "where honor and danger collide with love." She combines actual Texas settings with characters who are in realistic and dangerous situations. Angi has been a finalist for the Booksellers' Best Award, *RT Book Reviews* Best First Series, Gayle Wilson Award of Excellence and the Daphne du Maurier Award.

Angi and her husband live in North Texas, with only the four-legged "kids" left in the house to interrupt her writing. They recently began volunteering for a local Labrador foster program. Visit her website, www.angimorgan.com, or hang out with her on Facebook.

Books by Angi Morgan

HARLEQUIN INTRIGUE
1232—HILL COUNTRY HOLDUP
1262—.38 CALIBER COVER-UP
1406—DANGEROUS MEMORIES
1423—PROTECTING THEIR CHILD
1471—THE MARINE'S LAST DEFENSE
1495—NAVY SEAL SURRENDER*

*Texas Family Reckoning

CAST OF CHARACTERS

Lieutenant John Sloane—On leave from the navy SEALs, he returns home after twelve years to help with the care of his father and reunite with his identical twin brother. He soon discovers just how dire the situation is for the Double Bar Ranch.

Alicia Adams—Widow, mother, at-home nurse and high school sweetheart of John. Can she forgive him for leaving without a word twelve years ago?

Brian Sloane—John's identical estranged twin. Thinking his brother guilty, he accepted the blame for an accident that could have destroyed both their lives. Their small town has never forgiven him.

J.W. Sloane—Widower and owner of the Double Bar Ranch and father to the adult twins. He's recovering from a major stroke.

Dwayne Adams—Amy's deceased husband, who tragically lost his life in a car accident when their daughter was six months old. He was also Brian's best friend in high school.

Roy Adams—Dwayne's father, who is said to have died from a broken heart at the loss of his son.

Shauna and Patrick Weber—Only a few years older than Dwayne, Shauna married Roy Adams, and soon after his death, married Patrick.

Mary Fitz—Runs the town day care. The older woman has been a friend to Amy her entire life.

Mabel Standridge—Owns a house next to the Sloane Double Bar Ranch and helps the brothers with the care of J.W.

Chapter One

Join the navy. See the world.

"I don't think they meant the sandboxes I've been playing in." John Sloane had met and helped a lot of great people around the world. He'd been to several cool cities, nice ports and seen a lot of water. But he never wanted to see most of the places his unit had been deployed again—even in the news.

Back in Texas. Right back where he'd started wasn't exactly what he'd had in mind when he was eighteen. But right now he didn't care about choices or destinations. He just wanted information on his dad.

He'd returned from a training exercise and was told that his father had suffered a major stroke. When he couldn't reach the house or his dad, he'd called the police station with no luck. They'd refused to help.

From the message, he knew that his father was alive and at the ranch. He'd arranged extended leave and a ticket back to his hometown. Taking as much time off as he wanted wasn't a problem. He had a lot stored up. He wanted to be here as long as needed to get his father back on his feet. The only objective so far was to get home.

Two hours in triple-digit heat with the rental's AC whacked-out had added to his building frustration. He was sailing blind with no information, since his brother hadn't returned his calls and the home phone seemed to be out of order.

If John was being honest—no sense lying to himself—he hadn't been the most dependable brother. Or the most communicative. Since they'd learned to open their mouths, Brian had been the twin to tell the world what they needed. Brian had been the responsible one keeping him out of trouble, right up to his last words to him, "Leave and never look back."

That was exactly what he'd done.

John had followed through on his promise, joined the navy, left the ranch and had never come back.

In the navy, he wasn't Brian's twin or Johnny Junior or the baby. He'd quickly risen to chief petty officer and was the man you went to with a problem. He was the guy who got things done. Action, not words.

Then things changed. Promotions after online classes and a college degree. Instead of solving the problems, he followed orders. Now a lieutenant, he was the man responsible if someone got shot. A man who'd been doing too much thinking recently.

Texas? California? Navy? Private sector? Which road should just simple *John* choose? Too much thinking…. Right now he would help his dad, work the horses and maybe—just maybe—reconnect with his brother. That was the mission.

Deciding his future could wait.

His hometown was just ahead, and suddenly he didn't feel so confident. Since that short good riddance right after graduation, he hadn't seen or spoken to Brian. John hadn't seen his father in almost three years. How would the town see him now? Who would he be after twelve years? The man he'd become, or the kid the town remembered?

Aubrey looked like a busy small town instead of the bus-stop intersection with one red light he'd left. Lots of changes, and yet the most familiar thing in the world to him. He knew what stool old man Searcy would be sitting on for his lunch at the café, and he knew who would be serving him his blue-plate special. His stomach growled, emphasizing his lack of lunch. Another ten minutes and he'd be home.

Home.

The word felt good. He'd stay, help his dad around the ranch, work with his back instead of a weapon. He'd welcome every minute of mind-numbing grunt labor. And somehow he'd figure out what to do with the rest of his life.

He raised a finger off the steering wheel, acknowledging those driving past. A friendly custom in north Texas, like tipping your hat. Or at least it used to be. People stared at him and quickly looked away when he caught their eye. He drove through his little town, now full of fast-food restaurants and an outdoor mini shopping mall. He turned off the main road, took the familiar turns and passed the mailbox—faded with one of the letters missing from his father's name.

Parked on the side of the driveway was a cherry-red Camaro. A car he knew inside and out. The car had always hummed perfection. Mark Miller had won many drag races with that engine. When Mark had left for the army, John had tried to buy it from Mr. Miller many times. He slowed as the driver—obviously waiting on him—opened the door of the car he'd wanted throughout his teenage years. His tires crunched on the gravel as he pulled to a stop.

"Wow." The word slipped from his brain to his mouth.

"You still haven't gotten over this car?" the woman said, caressing the hood with long strokes.

Thankfully, she thought he was gawking at the muscle car. The vehicle was a nice backdrop to the curvy medium-height babe with long wavy dark brown hair and eyes hidden behind aviator shades.

Dressed in old worn jeans that hugged her hips and a tank top that hugged everything else, he couldn't focus on the car if he wanted to.

And he really didn't want to. If he had air-conditioning, he would have cranked it to high. Instead, the sweat beaded on his forehead. He grabbed the button-up shirt he'd tossed on the seat next to him to wipe his face.

"Driving with the windows down? Braving the Texas heat, Johnny? You forget how hot it gets here in July?" the babe asked, crossing the road in worn boots. She slid her glasses to the top of her head, tucking her hair back in the process. Bright smiling eyes laughed at him.

"Alicia?" He recognized her voice, but none of the curves she currently sported.

"Welcome home." She leaned on the open window, giving him a great view straight between her breasts. A much better view than he'd ever seen in high school.

"How did you know I'd be here?"

"I was already at the house. Wanda thought she saw Brian in a new car and sent a text asking if he'd come into some cash." She shrugged her bare, tanned shoulders. "I knew Brian was in the barn. So I assumed and waited." She stepped back, pulling the door open. "Get out here so I can give you a proper welcome home. It's been a while."

Alicia Miller, now Adams. Or had she gone back

to Miller after her husband had died? Either way, he barely recognized his high school sweetheart. She'd definitely filled out in all the right places. He popped the seat-belt release and stood, towering over her in a white undershirt that probably smelled as bad as the horse stalls. She wrapped her arms around his middle and squeezed. He hugged her back.

Home.

They separated, and the pearly-white smile he expected was gone. He missed her hand swinging upward, until it connected with his cheek. Connected hard. He rubbed it, not ashamed to let her know the slap had stung. Caught off guard by a girl. Or maybe he deserved it. Time enough to contemplate later.

A fitting welcome home.

"Before you ask, that was for your dad. J.W. will never say or do anything to make you feel ashamed, but you deserve that and more for just leaving. It broke his heart."

The little fireball choked on the last word. But she was right. And he was grown enough now to admit he'd made a mistake by not calling more often. "You've seen him? Is he okay?"

"He gets stronger every day. I'm his nurse and help him with physical therapy. That's what I do, at-home nursing."

"Just for the record, that's the one and only time

you'll slap me and get away with it." He leaned against the rear door, crossing his arms to keep them in check. He didn't know if he wanted to drive away or reach out and pull her back to fill the emptiness he suddenly experienced.

"Are you okay? I didn't mean to hurt you. I'm not even sure why I did that. I never do that. And now I'm just babbling."

"Really?" Had it been too long to tease her? She'd been a junior in college the last time he'd heard anything. Their lives had changed when he hadn't chosen that route. Really changed when Brian had taken the blame for the accident. They hadn't spoken since his twin had accused him of being irresponsible and leaving a campfire burning.

After boot camp, his dad said Brian had decided not to attend college. Brian's taking public blame for the fire meant John could achieve his dream of entering the navy. It wouldn't have happened otherwise, and he owed his brother his entire career.

Join the navy. See the world.

It had been his dream, and his brother had pushed him toward it, sacrificing everything to let him keep it. *That* was the problem. The closest people to him had believed the accusation.

"I should be…" She gestured toward her car. "Your father's waiting."

"You said Brian was in the barn?"

"He was earlier." Alicia stuck her hands into her

front pockets, creating a shrug whether she wanted one or not. "Sorry I slapped you, Johnny."

"I'm sorry you needed to." He rubbed his cheek again, scraping the three days of growth.

Alicia took a step toward him, awkwardly pulled him down for what he thought was another hug. He didn't reach for her. Instead, supersoft fingers caressed him from the bottom of his ears down both lines of his jaws. The sting disappeared faster than a radar blip.

Before he could react, she'd kissed his lips, lingering just a second too long for it to be just a friendly welcome home. Then she waved and returned to her car.

"See you around."

The dust from the road stuck to his arms and face as he stood there like an idiot while she drove away.

"Wow."

The Double Bar had been around for over a hundred years, supplying its fair share of cutting horses and rodeo stock. Oak trees had towered over the winding gravel driveway, since just after the Civil War. They'd formed a canopy and should have been a sight for his weary eyes. It was normally one of the coolest places on the ranch. The trees stretching above his head looked gnarly. Had anyone trimmed them since he'd left? He had to slow to avoid the potholes. The pasture looked more like West Texas desert than grazing potential for a herd.

"What the hell's happened?"

Granddad's old Dodge truck was loaded with feed and supplies. No doubt his work would start this afternoon, no waiting around. The ranch never let you take a vacation. John parked the rental, dropped the tailgate of the truck and slapped a bag.

Wham. Slammed to the ground, he spit dirt from his mouth. A punch to his kidney caused him to tighten his gut and pull his arms tight against his sides. The attacker shuffled off and away. John scrambled to his knees and popped up to both feet.

"You've got a lot of nerve showing up now!"

"Brian? What the…" He wiped the dirt from his face just in time to block a punch. His hands automatically formed fists. He resisted throwing his right at the last minute, but his shoulder momentum took him a step closer to his brother. "Cut it out or find yourself on the ground."

"Yeah, who's going to put me there? Oh, right, the son who's been gone twelve years. Think you can take me with all your fancy military training?"

John couldn't start his return home by teaching Brian a lesson. He relaxed his body enough to appear nonthreatening, but didn't lose eye contact. Brian would always give his punches away by dropping his gaze to the ground before he swung. Better to avoid being hit than make things worse by hitting back.

"Come on, man, I just got here," he said. Home

for fifteen minutes and already he'd been slapped and eaten a face full of dirt. His lower back didn't feel all that great, either.

"That's the point. Dad's stroke was over a week ago."

"No excuses. I was on a mission and got here as soon as I could. How is he?"

"Busy saving strangers and can't be bothered at home." Brian grabbed a fifty-pound bag of feed, throwing it to his shoulder like a bulky pillow, then stomped toward the shed. "Go see for yourself. Alicia usually leaves him in front of the television."

Guess it wasn't the right time to remind his brother he'd called a couple of dozen times in the past two days. John rubbed his side, then his jaw, and dusted some of the dirt from his body. *What a welcome.*

"Dad?" He pushed the screen door open with the hesitation of entering the unknown. He didn't know what to expect. Light on his feet, soundlessly moving through the kitchen and sitting room, he was afraid of what he'd find in front of the loud television.

A severe stroke ten days ago when he'd been working horses. That's all John knew. He'd left messages on his dad's cell, but no one had called back. His dad kept him up-to-date. Sad, but he didn't know his brother's number.

Bad communication skills were nothing new

before he'd left for the navy. More bad habits had formed when he'd been in training and not allowed to call. Then long missions with no communication. Different time zones. Easy after that to avoid calling home by just being too busy—or pretending to be. His father had accepted the excuses. His brother had told him never to look back and meant it.

He was a different man. They both were. They had time to fix what was wrong. Later.

Right now it was about his dad—who was asleep in a wheelchair in a room that no longer resembled his mother's favorite in the house. Full of a hospital bed, pulleys, a portable toilet and other medical stuff, everything familiar had been removed. There was a flat-screen TV hanging on the wall.

He heard the water running in the kitchen behind him and jerked around, surprised Brian had entered without making a sound.

"Dad, wake up." Brian shoved a shoulder into John as he passed. His angry twin turned a gentle hand to touch their dad's shoulder and not startle him awake. "John's home."

He understood the pain. His brother had a right to be upset, from the serious look of things. He'd been here taking care of the ranch and their dad. Alone.

The last time they'd been face-to-face, they were skinny kids eating their dad out of a ton of groceries. Identical twins who could have passed for each other—and had fooled more than a teacher or two. Not to mention the girls. There were differences now. The most obvious was their hair. His was the navy regulation, high and tight over his ears. Brian's was longish, touching his collar.

John knew the tense jaw-clenching muscle all too well. Strange seeing what it looked like to others. Their bodies were toned from different types of exercises—his PT and Brian's ranch work. Weird that they still looked so much alike.

"I got here as soon as I could. I had no idea," John apologized. He would not complain about the lack of information provided by his brother. It would just upset his dad.

"That's an understatement," Brian mumbled.

His dad shook his head. Upset. Brian patted his shoulder. "I know, Dad. I told you I'd explain things when he got here."

He kept his mouth shut, stunned at the fright he saw in his father's eyes. The stroke had left him paralyzed. He couldn't talk. Brian lifted a straw to the left side of his dad's mouth and patiently waited, that angry gleam still in his eyes when he connected with John.

"Dad had a stroke and was lucky to survive. Recovery's going to take a while, but he's doing great." He put the mug on the table. "Looks like Alicia wore you out as usual, old man. Time for a nap, right?"

Brian moved swiftly. John moved in to help but was waved off. In two shakes, J. W. Sloane was back in bed. Brian maneuvered him quickly and with the same calm ease he handled troubled animals.

"I got this. Go get cleaned up and I'll get him settled. I'm sure you have things to explain."

Things hadn't changed; his brother issued orders for him to follow. And just like every day of his life, he followed orders well. Stowing his gear back in a room that hadn't changed except for the layers of dust, he wondered if the day would ever come where he'd be deciding his *own* fate.

Chapter Two

"Hey, beautiful."

"Mommy! Mommy! Look, I'm a princess."

Alicia Ann Adams watched her four-year-old daughter run across the playroom, dodging toys and playmates. Her yellow sunflower dress had a purple stain on the front—most likely grape jam from a snack. She lifted her over the gate guard in her day-care room to squeeze her close. "What did you do today?"

"We painted and dressed up. I was a princess and gots to wear the crown all the time."

"Well, that was appropriate for my very own Princess Lauren. Did you put your toys away?"

"The other girls are still playing with everything, Alicia. Don't worry about it this time."

She put Lauren down, dreading the next part of the conversation. "Go pick up a bit, sweetie. I need to talk with Miss Mary."

"Is something wrong?" asked the woman responsible for her daughter's daily care.

Mary Fitz had owned and run the day care forever. Alicia had stayed here before starting kindergarten, and had worked here in high school. There was nowhere else she wanted her daughter to stay. Which made not being able to pay Mary all the more difficult.

"I'm afraid tomorrow's our last day. It isn't fair to ask you to let Lauren stay when I can't pay you, Mary." What was she going to do? She couldn't take Lauren with her to her clients' homes, and she had to work.

"Nonsense. I've told you before just pay me when you can. I trust you. I know what you're going through. Working on your own to spend more time with your daughter is admirable, dear. Starting this place wasn't easy, either. Everyone thought I was a crazy widow. So don't fret. She's safe here." Mary turned back to the children. "Lauren, time to go, sweetheart."

Alicia was going to cry. She hadn't been able to think of Dwayne without all the problems he'd left when he'd died four years ago. Leaving her with a newborn and without a will had created chaos in a once-happy life. Those thoughts seemed utterly ridiculous compared to his death. Nevertheless, they were true.

The tears were building, so she pressed the palms of her hands to her closed eyes, attempting to stop the waterworks. Mary had saved her life. Again.

"It won't be too long. I have to drive a bit farther, but there are two more patients in Sanger."

"It's really not a problem, Alicia. I'm glad to help." She lifted Lauren over the doorway gate. "She had so much fun playing princess today. Such an imagination. Keep the crown, sweetie."

"Say bye-bye to Miss Mary." They both waved to one of the nicest people left in their lives. "See you tomorrow."

Unfortunately, she wasn't branching out on her own willingly like Mary thought. She'd been forced to resign from the Denton hospital.

After years with a spotless record, her patients' exit questionnaires were suddenly full of mysterious complaints. Complaints that had all begun at the same time Dwayne's trust fund was frozen and her mother-in-law sought control.

Coincidence?

And then an anonymous caller said they'd witnessed her selling drugs. *Anonymous? Not hardly. It has to be Shauna.*

She'd never believed anyone could be that cruel. Especially family. She didn't *want* to believe Shauna, her mother-in-law, was responsible for the loss of her job at Denton Regional. But if she hadn't been, she wouldn't have known about Alicia's dismissal and wouldn't have filed for custody of Lauren the same day.

Ugh. I certainly wish I wasn't forced to refer to her as my mother-in-law.

Dwayne had never called Shauna Weber his step-mother. She was the same age and had even gone on a couple of dates with him their junior year. She'd married a man two years younger only four months after Dwayne's father had died.

Think about the extra time you have with Lauren today.

With only a couple of home clients on her Monday schedule, she should be rejoicing about the light load and playing with her daughter. But a light load meant light money. Next on her list was to speak with her landlord. He'd be upset splitting the rent again, but her paychecks just weren't large enough for her to get a couple of weeks ahead.

A real shame they couldn't head straight to the park, but it was 107 degrees outside. Almost as hot in the car, even with the AC on high. Store first, then dinner, then a cooler playtime on the swings before her bath.

It was hard to enjoy anything. She was still shaking. Money—or the lack of it—always got her this way. Then throw in what happened with Johnny and she was a nervous wreck.

How in the world had she ever thought she could welcome him home? She could still feel the sting of that slap on her hands. Feel the strength in his arms around her waist. Feel the tingle down her spine from kissing him.

She glanced in the rearview mirror to watch Lauren playing in her car seat.

It had been a major mistake kissing him. Really kissing him. Add a shot of guilt and disloyalty to her deceased husband, and her hands wouldn't stop shaking. If Johnny didn't know how she felt about his return before—he did now. Well, there was always the possibility he might be as thickheaded as when he'd left. Was he the only thing she could think about?

"Great. Just great. I was not supposed to kiss him. Ugh."

"Like a princess kisses a frog, Mommy?"

"Just like that, sweetie. Mommy did kiss a frog today, but he didn't turn into a prince. What do you want for dinner?" *Think about the park. And ice cream. Real ice cream from the Creamery. That would be nice. Getting cool. Don't think about the money or Johnny Sloane.*

"Chicken nuggets."

"You want those every night." She laughed at the nightly conversation.

It was definitely hard not to think about how great her high school boyfriend had looked. And felt. He'd been a solid rock under her hands. Why it seemed he was taller than Brian, she didn't understand, but it did. Not once, for as long as she'd known the Sloane brothers, had she been attracted to Brian. They'd never been able to fool her like they had so many of their teachers and friends.

Nope, she could always tell them apart.

She liked how John's hair was short over his ears, but not cropped completely down to the skin like it had been the last time she'd seen him. He looked fantastic. Strong. Sturdy. Like a man. She'd been thinking about him all day and had to stop.

It was Lauren time.

"I like nuggets. McDonald's nuggets." Her daughter giggled again.

Probably the dinner menu on those rare visits alone with a babysitter—without her mother-in-law's supervision. She turned into the store parking lot.

"How 'bout chicken nuggets from scratch? We have lots of time today, but first a stop at the store."

It didn't take long to get down the street to the grocery. She parked by the far basket return, always protecting her father's Camaro from dings and scratches. "Looks like you'll get to ride in your favorite play shopping cart. There aren't too many people here."

"Can we get real chocolate milk?"

"We have the stuff at home to mix it up."

"But Grandpa Weber's gots real chocolate milk straight from the cows," her daughter whined, sounding just like Shauna. How was that possible at the age of four? And she wasn't even blood related.

"Honey, it doesn't come that way." She was forever correcting the things Shauna's husband, Patrick, assured Lauren were true.

Alicia went to the passenger side to get Lauren. Cool-looking cars were absolutely not family cars. She pulled down the front seat and removed the shoulder restraints from Lauren, who waved to someone passing by.

"Hi," Lauren said.

Shoved just as she'd lifted Lauren, they both fell into the car. Her feet were kicked from under her. She couldn't stand.

"Somebody help!"

Thick material was yanked over her head, smelling like a burlap feed sack. She couldn't see. The pressure in her back grew sharp, like a knee. It moved to her neck. Someone forced her face into the hot leather. Lauren screamed behind her, kicking her side as she was dragged from the car.

They were taking her baby!

"Stop hurting my mommy," Lauren screamed.

"What do you want?"

Pushing. Shaking. Choking her from behind. She couldn't move. *Dear Lord in heaven, please send someone to help me.*

"Mommy!"

"Shh," a deep voice said.

Lauren continued a muffled scream.

"Please don't…don't hurt her. It'll be okay, baby."

"Shut up," a second gravelly voice whispered close to her ear. Her hands were quickly taped behind her.

"Don't do this. Please," she pleaded.

Shoved into the back floorboard, her boots removed, her ankles taped. She heard the lock being pushed down. The door slammed. The windows had been up. The keys were in her pocket. It was a scorching triple-digit day outside, but she was not going to die!

They'd kidnapped her little girl.

She felt the adrenaline rush through her body, but still couldn't tear the tape from her hands. She closed her eyes from the grain dust and shifted closer to the window. Then kicked and kicked some more. But the bastards had pulled off her boots and left her with only socks. Her heels couldn't touch the glass, just her toes. It was doubtful she could break the glass, but someone would hear the pounding.

Someone would see her. They'd call the police. They could break the window and get her out. Something. Something fast so they'd find Lauren.

Who could do this? She'd never give up until she found her daughter.

Sweat beaded over her face, making it itch. It was hard to breathe without inhaling the feed dust left in the sack. She choked, coughed, gagged. All the while twisting and using the carpet to slowly work the suffocating material from the bottom part of her face.

Kick. Keep kicking.

Don't stop.

"Don't. Give. Up. On me. Baby!"

Kick.

"Help! Can anybody hear me?"

Try to sit up. Impossible. She couldn't twist enough and was hooked to something. "The seat belt." They'd taped her hands to the front seat-belt strap.

Kick.

"Help." The dry, hoarse whisper was all she had left.

The tears wanted to come. They started. But it was so hot in the car she could barely catch her breath. *No tears.*

Kick.

Kick again.

A customer will bring their cart to the return. Someone would hear her. She just had to keep kicking. Someone would wonder why her dad's car was here. Wouldn't they?

Kick. *God, let me kick.*

Lauren....

Chapter Three

"No witnesses. No physical evidence. No ransom demand. The Amber Alert is still active. But it's been thirty-two hours since the kidnapping, and we've got nothing, Alicia."

County Sheriff Coleman had escorted her home from the hospital after recovering from heat stroke. Thank heavens someone had seen her through the window after she'd passed out. The excessive heat inside the car could have killed her. She'd hated to call the county sheriff to bring her home, but the press had made it impossible for her to leave unescorted, and the Aubrey police had refused to help.

Now he stood in her humble living/dining room like he had a dozen times in the past four years. Same humble sheriff, just a different house than when he'd notified her Dwayne had died at the scene of his car accident.

"I don't understand. We both know the only person who could be behind this is Shauna. She's publicly threatened to take Lauren from me." Her husband's stepmother had put on a good distraught act for the television cameras, but Alicia knew the truth.

Knew the Webers wanted her little girl's trust fund. Knew in her heart they were involved with the abduction. The gleam of dollar signs in their eyes proved it to her over and over again.

"Why can't anyone see past the fake tears she has only when the press is around?" There was something else just behind Shauna's heavy-lidded eyes. Gloating. The same look she'd had when they'd successfully frozen all of Dwayne's assets.

"Lauren isn't at the ranch or the Frisco house, where Shauna lives now. We've checked. We've followed Weber. We've searched every property remotely associated with either of them." The sheriff shook his head as he had each time he'd told her the same results while she'd been in the hospital.

"What about the FBI? Did you contact the Texas Rangers like you said? Or are you telling me to give up?" She wouldn't.

"I'm telling you I won't stop looking, but there's little I can do. The rangers are on watch and are conducting the investigation. They feel like this is a domestic dispute and haven't called in the FBI yet."

"Did Shauna stop them? Does everyone believe her and the lies she's telling the press? I did *not* kidnap my daughter for her trust fund." Vultures.

He hung his head, letting her assume it was true.

"It might be time for a private investigator," he said.

"I checked into them yesterday from the hospital. They all want a lot more money than I have access to. And they want it up front before they'll even begin." She went to the window to see if any cameras were still parked out front. None. "Shauna says she's hiring her own and swears if they find her, she'll take her away. Isn't that grounds for a search warrant or something? You've searched here based on the accusations of the press."

"Now, Alicia, that's not why the task force looked around and you know it. Shauna invited us to search all the property without a warrant."

"You know that in the media, I've already been found guilty of kidnapping my own daughter, but I'm not sure how I did it. I think of all the times I judged those mothers being crucified by the news stations. You never hear about them being found innocent. But I'll take the blame, Sheriff. I'll let them call me whatever they want to get Lauren home safely."

If she wasn't so tired, she'd pace the carpet. Sitting and waiting was driving her crazy. Too exhausted to stand any longer, she fell into the chair and couldn't stop the tears.

Lauren was gone and there was no one to find

her. The light pat on her back reminded her that the sheriff was politely waiting.

"Alicia, you know that wasn't me. I don't think you're using Lauren for publicity."

"I don't know what to do, Ralph." She needed to pull herself together one more time so he could leave. "Sorry I had to call you again, but I couldn't get out of the hospital door with those vultures wanting a statement."

The press had hounded her, comparing her to a desperate, unstable woman. Implying she'd kidnapped her own little girl for the ransom. The local newspaper had made the first insinuations in their weekly editorial. Reporting that she was broke, unable to pay her bills because she was in the process of suing her sweet mother-in-law for Lauren's trust fund.

"It's all so stupid crazy, Ralph. If anyone is hungry for cash, it's Shauna. Everyone knows she married Dwayne's dad for the money. Goodness, she was the same age as her stepson. She hated me in high school and especially hated me after I married Dwayne. Even more after Roy left everything in a trust to Lauren."

Another slow, awkward pat.

Pull it together.

"You should go. I'm fine. Really," she finally managed.

"Lock the doors, Alicia. I don't think it's safe."

She nodded, but if the kidnappers had wanted to kill her, it would have been much easier when they'd taken her baby. As it was, they were successfully framing her for their actions.

"I mean it, girl. They may be back to finish what they started. You could have died from being locked in that car."

"I'm fine." She feared her own neighbors more. That people she'd known all her life might take a mob mentality and throw bricks through her windows. Hadn't that happened to a mother of another kidnapped little girl?

"As long as you stay inside, you'll be fine." He patted her shoulder again, following with a little squeeze before heading to the door. "Lauren will be fine, too. We'll find her. I promise you that."

"Without any idea where she's been taken? Who's really looking?"

He dipped his head again, raised his hat to his head and stood on the outside of the screen, tapping the doorknob.

Alone. No one to hold on to.

Alicia dropped her face into her hands. "What am I going to do?"

"Find someone without connections to the Webers," he said through the glass, still waiting and pointing until she locked the door.

The silence was deafening after his car pulled away. How many nights over the past three and

a half years had she begged for a moment alone?
With no responsibility? Each moment spent away
from Lauren, she'd been working doubles at the
hospital. And now? Just one sweet giggle asking
for another drink of water. That was all she wanted
to hear.

She wiped more tears and stood straight. What
she needed was money. Shauna had Lauren hidden
somewhere. She watched the sheriff drive away
and turned the dead bolt. Money would help her
find her daughter.

Shc had to break her promise and sell her dad's
Camaro. There was one person who might want it
just as badly as she did.

Johnny.

"YOU CAN'T AVOID this forever. I've already given
him his meds. Next round is written on the schedule. He needs his exercises after lunch." Brian
grabbed his gym bag off the back porch and tossed
it over his shoulder. "I've got to go."

"Where are you headed?" John asked, letting the
screen slam behind him. He wanted Brian to answer
the question instead of ignoring him like he had
since he'd returned. Other than instructions about
their dad, Brian hadn't said anything except "pass
the butter," at breakfast. John's brother worked from
sunup till past midnight every day, breaking only
for meals and to take care of their dad.

And now he was taking off to go to "work" for four days?

"All you need to know is written down. Since Alicia can't be here, call Mabel if you need something."

"Shouldn't we hire another nurse or a proper physical therapist?" His brother's announcement last night that it was John's turn to take care of their dad had thrown him for a loop. He had no training for this sort of duty.

Helping his father—other than in and out of the wheelchair—wasn't like facing down the enemy. But for some reason making a mistake scared him to death.

"I won't do that to Alicia. And neither will you." Brian shook his head, adding to the disgust already plain on his face. "Truth is, we can't afford it. Dad doesn't have insurance. Alicia's been coming by without payment until I get some cash. She insisted. I'll pay her eventually, but I have to sell one of the mares. I've been having problems, since she's in Dad's name."

"I can pay. How much do you need?"

"Keep your money."

"It's for Dad," John said, stopping before he spouted what he really thought about his brother's pride.

Things were a lot worse than John had imagined, but even then, his brother's loyalty to Alicia wasn't a battle he was willing to wage. *Stick to Brian's plan and negotiate peace when the time is right.*

"Four days. Then we'll suffer through a discussion," Brian grudgingly mumbled.

The ranch and his dad were a different story. Brian couldn't keep him from looking at the financials while he was gone to "work."

"I'm not sure of what to do with Dad."

"There's a list of exercises on the stand next to his bed. It will give you a chance to talk to him without me around. You can complain all you want." Brian shoved his hair off his face and pulled an old beat-up straw hat onto his head. "Mabel said she's glad to help with Dad and is five minutes across the road."

"I remember where Mrs. Standridge lives. Why are you wearing Dad's hat?" His brother shot him a look and stuffed the hat harder on his head. "You could drive the rental to wherever you're headed. I don't have to return it for another couple of days."

"Now, why would I want to do that?" He tossed his gym bag into the front of the truck and climbed in. "Don't call her unless you really need to impose."

"Don't impose. Right," John mumbled to a trail of dust mixed with gas fumes. "Four days without a freaking clue. Is that a reason to impose?"

Talking to his brother was more difficult than facing a terrorist. Brian was right about one thing—

speaking to his dad had always been easy. But that was a long time ago, before two-minute conversations or voice-mail tag had become their routine. Long before his dad had such a hard, frustrating time just communicating that he wanted a sip of water. Maybe he could talk about some of his war stories? His dad might enjoy those.

But storytelling would have to wait until he'd checked forty sets of hooves. Made certain the rest of the herd was moved to the front pasture—what was left of it—and had plenty of water. Checked the fence line, which meant saddling an unfamiliar horse and riding for the first time in twelve years. In between the three-page to-do list, he was supposed to check on his father every half hour.

How had Brian kept up with the work four hired men had accomplished while they'd been growing up? And why had he left with only a small bag for four days?

Well, if Brian could do it, he could do it. He *wanted* to do it. If he could handle hotheaded naval aviators, he could handle some chores he'd done most of his childhood.

Piece of cake.

Chapter Four

He couldn't do it.

Saddle sore, John wanted to drop in a chair, turn on a mind-numbing rerun of an old television show and drink a beer. If he'd been in San Diego, that was exactly what he would be doing. Or hitting the beach.

Of course, if he'd been at home in front of his TV, he wouldn't be frustrated at not completing any task on Brian's list. He'd consistently been aware of each minute slithering by. The stops and starts of checking on his dad had disrupted each job he'd begun. As a result, he hadn't finished anything.

After a couple of hours he'd admitted he was out of his element. He'd run and trained almost every day since leaving home, but every part of him was sore in a different way. By lunch he'd called Mrs. Standridge. He wasn't ashamed to ask for help. He was used to teamwork, admitting his shortcomings and working to improve.

As soon as she'd arrived, he'd seen the look in

his dad's eyes change. Brian could have been a little more specific that their father was embarrassed for anyone to see him. Mable had let him know a couple of hours ago she'd fed his dad breakfast for a late lunch, something J.W. could eat almost on his own. J.W. clearly didn't want her in the house, but there wasn't a choice. They needed help.

The excruciating one-hundred-plus temperature had climbed along with the sun. By the heat of the afternoon, it had hit 109. Might just make it down to ninety-eight later that night. Finally some relief. Ha! He hadn't experienced a Texas summer since his teens. He'd like to see Brian survive after being dropped in the middle of a desert, dressed in full gear. He missed the ocean breeze and his run along the beach in California.

Different life. Time to concentrate on this one and see if Brian would allow him to return home more often. Yeah, he was seeking permission from his brother.

Which meant getting inside and tackling more things on the list. But first, he needed to get some of the sweat off him. One bathroom meant no shower until Mabel left. He crossed to the watering trough he'd just filled, pulled his shirt off and stuck his head under. The water cooled him like the shock of jumping in the Pacific.

He shook his head and swiped his hand over his face to sluice the water off before he headed to the house. The distinct hum of his favorite Camaro pulled behind him and stopped.

The last person he'd expected to see was Alicia. When he turned, there she was, one hand gripping the steering wheel, one hand gripping her cell. She didn't make a move to get out of the car. According to the news he'd just heard, her kid was still missing. Why was she here?

Lost. He'd seen that look before.

The petrified stare of someone who had no options.

"Alicia?" He opened the car door, reached across and turned the engine off then leaned on the roof. "Hey, you okay?"

"No."

A whisper of desperation. Tears trickling from swollen eyes. She barely resembled the confident woman who'd met him in the driveway.

"They can't find her and…"

"I want to help, but I'm not certain what I can do."

He could see her trying to keep control by blowing air through her puffed cheeks. It wasn't working. Again, out of his element. Should he get her out of the car and take her inside or bring Mabel out here?

"They— I thought— I have to sell the car, but he just called…." She shook her head. Tears streamed from her red-rimmed eyes. "They've arrested him."

"Who? Did they find your daughter?"

"No. It was— Brian just called."

"Is Brian buying the car? He's not here." He should get Mabel. Maybe she could understand and tell him what this was all about.

Alicia turned to him, took a deep breath before she made eye contact. "They arrested Brian for Lauren's kidnapping."

ALICIA LOOKED AROUND the faded yellow kitchen in the Sloane house. She'd spent lots of summer days with the twins' mother here. Waiting on fresh lemonade or homemade peanut-butter cookies. More recently, she'd spent time cooking simple meals for J.W. and Lauren while Brian handled ranch stuff.

Or at least she'd thought he'd been handling ranch stuff.

Of course he was. Don't start doubting him. He's not the kidnapper or a drug dealer like half the town thinks. Shauna's behind the kidnapping. You just have to prove she's guilty.

"Here you go, dear. I have dinner for you both whenever you're ready."

"Thanks, Mabel. I'm not really hungry." Alicia took a cool wet cloth and placed it over her eyes. She was so tired of thinking. So tired of trying to decide how or where to start.

"Did you find out anything?" John asked.

"Well, that silly receptionist or whoever they

have answering the phones said they won't let anyone talk to Brian until after he's been formally charged." Mabel continued to move around the kitchen as she spoke. "I wanted to send Dave Krueger over for representation, but they told her Brian didn't want a lawyer and then mentioned your brother was being cheap and stubborn."

"I can't believe Brian refused a lawyer or that the situation has spun out of control so rapidly." *Cheap and stubborn.* She totally understood those two words. She heard Johnny grunt from the doorway. "Did they arrest him based on an anonymous tip?"

"That's why they initially pulled him over. Then they found Lauren's toys behind the seat," Mabel said, patting her shoulder once and moving away.

Alicia used her palms to keep the cloth in place. Her eyes were swollen and burning from the constant crying. "We told her not to play in the truck. This is all my fault he's in jail."

"No, dear, it's not," Mabel said. "And tomorrow morning he'll be charged or free. I'll make certain he has a good lawyer whether he wants one or not."

"I'm so glad you're here for J.W.," she told Mabel, removing the cool cloth and feeling calmer just sitting at the old dining table. Her insides still shook, but she could talk rationally again. The anxiety wouldn't leave until Lauren was back safe and sound.

"I am, too." John's deep voice rumbled softly

through the room. "Thanks for calling the police station. I moved Dad back to bed. I'd like to see Brian ASAP. Can you stay? I hate to ask, but I'll probably need to be gone tomorrow as well if he's not released."

"Not a problem." Mabel folded the kitchen towel and laid it on the dish drain. "Let me run home and feed the dog. I believe the jail opens at eight in the morning. I'm an early riser but I don't think you'd want me at five, so I'll come at seven-thirty. Be right back."

Alicia replaced the washcloth against her face while Mabel gently shut the door and left. Hot air from outside drifted across the room. She didn't know how to look at this man. Or how to talk to him. Or how to apologize or explain her behavior. So much had happened since he'd left home, and he seemed to be clueless.

Where did she begin?

By looking at him.

She wiped her face one last time and set the cloth aside. He'd put a shirt on. His hair was still wet, but she'd heard the shower while Mabel had washed dishes.

"You doing okay?" John asked.

She watched by peeking through her fingers as he turned one of the old metal dining chairs away from the table, sat and leaned across the back.

"Brian sits exactly like that. But I'd never think you were him."

John's bland expression subtly switched to annoyance as he tapped the table. Easily spotted on a man who didn't really show much emotion.

"You and Brian a thing now?"

"No. It's not anything like that."

"Why don't you explain just how it is? If you're up to it." John didn't move. He was tall enough that when he sat in a chair he still seemed to tower over her. "You should probably start with why the police booked him for your daughter's kidnapping and why the first person he told was you."

"Shauna's responsible for the anonymous tip. I'm certain she's trying to frame Brian and me. Sheriff Coleman thinks so, too, even though he can't say that to anyone else."

"*Did* he say it to you?" John remained steady, his arms crossed over the top of the chair. His eyes constantly moved between her and his dad.

"No. But he didn't disagree when I said it. You need to take care of Brian. I just came to see if you wanted to buy the car."

"Shauna who? And why do you need money?"

"Shauna Weber was Dwayne's stepmother and the reason my accounts are frozen."

"Why would his stepmother freeze your assets?"

"Because she's a money-hungry bi— Sorry, I can't talk rationally about her. Look, Johnny, can you buy the car? I need money for a private investigator. It's the only way I'll ever find Lauren before Shauna pretends to find her and takes her away from me."

"That's quite an assumption, Alicia."

"I'm not assuming anything." Shoving the chair backward, it hit the kitchen wall. She was losing it. She forced herself to sit and take cleansing breaths before she babbled again. She couldn't look at him to see what he thought of her outburst and couldn't imagine why he wasn't lecturing her, like anyone else she'd tried to confide in. "It's the only explanation. Shauna has frozen Dwayne's assets, including Lauren's trust fund, and I...I just need the cash for the car. If you still want it, that is. Then I can get out of your hair."

"You mean the court froze everything," he corrected.

"Shauna took me to court. As if she has a right to any of that money. It belongs to my daughter. I hate having to use it, but it was our only support while the will was being contested. Now there's nothing except a few home-care clients who stuck with me."

Would he remember the same friendship they'd had as kids? Be sympathetic enough to give her more than the car's estimated value? She gathered her courage to make eye contact with him. But his gaze was toward the living area and his father.

"The house wasn't built for wheelchair access." She attempted to draw his attention again. "Brian set J.W.'s bed there so he could work here at the table and still see him."

"Back to Brian's arrest," he said, lowering his voice. "Why my brother? If you're just friends, what does he have to do with your daughter?"

"Shauna and Patrick Weber have made several accusations that we're having an affair. That we kidnapped Lauren for ransom."

"We. Meaning you and Brian. But there hasn't been a ransom note."

"One showed up last night at the Weber show barns. They tried to blame me, but didn't know I had a solid alibi. The sheriff was at my house. So they immediately accused Brian of working with me."

"That's ridiculous. He was out with the horses until after dark."

"The note was left at their stables that back up to your property line."

"You mean Pat Weber owns old man Adams's stables? He used to work there."

"Shauna married him four months after Dwayne's father died. If that doesn't prove she just wanted the money, I don't know what does. Marrying Roy Adams was another way she could get close to Dwayne after high school. With both of them gone, she's selling off everything."

"Wait. Are you talking about Shauna Tipton, the cheerleader a couple of years older than us? Didn't she date Dwayne? This sounds like a damn soap opera."

"Tell me about it. I've been living this nightmare for years. Brian's a good man. Shauna will use anything that can be taken out of context."

"Right. I still don't see why the police would arrest my brother. If there's nothing between you guys, how did they connect Brian to the kidnapping?"

"I've always been his friend and I stayed here with J.W. while Brian worked his four-day shift in Fort Worth last week."

"Shift?"

"He's a paramedic. Wasn't that where he was headed this morning when they arrested him?"

"He didn't mention where he was headed. Just that he'd be gone four days."

Spoken just like his brother. Same attitude, tone, inflection. If they tried to fool people, not many would be able to tell them apart. But she could. She also recognized the stubbornness that kept them from speaking to each other after Johnny left for the navy.

"I'm not reprising the role of mediator between you two. You can talk to him at the police station."

He nodded once. Curt, not rude. Just like he accepted her words and there was no need for any more. "That still doesn't explain why they'd think Brian kidnapped your daughter."

"Lauren. Her name is Lauren, and I want her home. She needs to be home with me." Fear blocked the last words, cutting them short.

"Do you know why they're assuming he took Lauren, tried to kill you and then just hung around the ranch until he was arrested?" He'd raised his voice just a tad and looked toward J.W., who still appeared to be sleeping far enough away not to hear the conversation. "It isn't a logical plan of attack and would mean that you involved a third person to hide Lauren somewhere. It doesn't make sense."

"They don't need a reason. There are townspeople who have been trying to send him to jail for twelve years."

John's brows drew together. He shook his head, compressed his lips and appeared genuinely confused.

"You don't know? You're Brian's twin and you're telling me you don't know what happened after you left?"

"Would I be asking if I did?" He sounded very annoyed.

Technically, he hadn't asked, but she saw the visible tick in his jaw muscle. He was obviously upset. She could barely believe her two best friends had grown so far apart. Identical twins who had shared secrets and pranks all through school.

"Brian admitted to starting the fire that killed Mrs. Cook."

"I know. He thought I caused the accident and took the blame."

There was some emotion Johnny couldn't hide. He stiffened and blinked his eyes a smidgen too long. They'd both changed over twelve years, but some things never would. The man sitting with her was just as hurt as the eighteen-year-old boy had been when his brother had believed the lies spread about the fire.

"They've never forgiven him."

"Who?" He looked genuine asking his question, like he really didn't have a clue.

"Everybody. Other than the sheriff, Mabel and me, no one talks to him. Ever. No one ever told you why he didn't go to A&M?"

"I assumed he changed his mind. Neither of us were good in school."

"But you knew he lost his scholarship, right?"

John's poker face melted.

"Your dad never said anything?"

"He didn't talk too much about Brian." John dropped his gaze to the tabletop.

"In other words, you didn't ask because you didn't want to hear."

"I'm listening now."

"The town was upset about Mrs. Cook's death. It didn't matter that it was an accident. They wanted

Brian punished. So there were outcries and editorials demanding consequences. Teachers withdrew their letters of recommendations."

"They could do that?" he asked in a hurt whisper.

"The university suddenly didn't have a full scholarship. They reduced it to about a thousand dollars. He couldn't finance the rest."

Disbelief, astonishment, anger—a ton of emotion took charge and marched across his face. "You can count on my help. Whatever it takes. We'll find your daughter and clear Brian."

"I don't know what you can do, John. The police and rangers have an Amber Alert. No one saw anything, no clues, no prints, no way to find her. It's like she just disappeared."

Alicia saw his fists tighten, ready to do battle to defend his family. It had been a while since she'd felt someone was completely on her side.

"I can help. Trust me."

The harsh tightness across his face softened. His hand took hers and she saw a glimpse of a friend. It had been a while since she'd depended on anyone. She nodded, realizing that trusting him was second nature. She'd run to the Double Bar because he was home.

Chapter Five

"Tell me what happened after I left and what we're up against." John paced the kitchen, keeping his dad's napping form in his peripheral vision. He didn't want him upset.

After the first couple of stories, John barely listened to Alicia's recounting of how the town had treated Brian. He was still stuck on his brother's arrest. Instead of calling a lawyer, Brian had phoned Alicia.

What was up with that? Was it his way of keeping his family informed without talking to John? Warning Alicia? She thought they were being framed. "Do the police know who Brian called?"

"I'm not sure." She looked as confused as he felt.

Cute and confused, with that worry line emphasized between her brows. Now wasn't the time for an attraction, and neither was the future. Alicia claimed there was nothing between her and Brian, and she thought they were only friends. They were clearly closer than either wanted to admit. They always had been.

"What did Brian say, exactly?"

She put her fingertips to her temples, concentrating. "They pulled him over, found Lauren's bear and crown behind his seat—the one I said she had with her when they…when they took her. The Aubrey police would be coming to the house to talk to me."

"You sort of buried the lead, Alicia. I think Brian called to warn you not to go home."

"Do you think they left something at my house?" She shook her head and her long hair fell forward, covering her face. "The media has already taken Shauna's side and is insinuating that I arranged for Lauren's kidnapping to get the ransom money. Do you believe they're going to arrest me? I haven't done anything."

He didn't have time to be sensitive, so blunt would have to work. "If Shauna's gone to the trouble to frame you for faking a kidnapping, don't you think they'd plant evidence to implicate you?" He let that info take root. "You've got two choices. Turn yourself in and hope it can all be sorted out legally."

She looked up, eyes wide with fright. "If I'm in jail, no one will be looking for Lauren."

John didn't correct her. Everyone had looked for

her daughter. To clear Brian, he would do more than just look. He'd find her. "Then hide."

"How can I hide? I don't have any money and I can't go anywhere. Dad's car is fairly easy to spot."

"I can help with that." He stood, glancing to the living room to verify his dad was still asleep. When he turned back, she stood touching distance in front of him. But she didn't reach out, and neither did he.

"Johnny, I can't ask you to help more than just buying the car. Your dad needs you."

"Don't bother, Alicia. You need my help. More important, the only way to clear Brian is to find your daughter. And I need *you* to make that happen."

"Thanks isn't enough." She launched herself and hugged him. "What should I do?"

John awkwardly set her away, not trusting himself to hold her close. The next few days were going to be hard enough. "We'll put your car in the shed, and if they look, I'll tell them you sold it to me."

"What's next?" She removed the key ring from her pocket, clutching it like a lifeline.

"Do you have a smartphone?"

"Yes."

"Book yourself on the next flight to San Antonio. Don't browse anything out of state. If the FBI's not involved yet, we want to keep the search for you in Texas. When you're done, take the battery out and leave it in Dad's things. Someplace you'd normally have access when you check on him."

"You want them to think I'm running. They won't believe it. They know I wouldn't go anywhere without Lauren."

"Did you think you'd be set up for her kidnapping?" He could see she was terrified. Her daughter had been abducted. Even if she was certain of who took her, there was still a deep fear of making a mistake. Doubt that she could be wrong.

It happened to him on every mission. Especially the ones that cost a man's life. Questioning your decisions would drive you insane. So you couldn't question. Someone like Alicia needed someone to help make those decisions. As long as he was around to take the blame, she wouldn't have to question if *she* did the right thing.

"And what if they release Brian or if asking me questions would help them find where Lauren is?"

"I don't know if they have enough evidence to hold Brian. They might release him, watch who he contacts, hoping they're right and that he'll lead them to the person holding your daughter. But more important, I need you with me to find Lauren."

"You really think this is the best way? Running?"

"Hiding. Staying under wraps until we gather all the facts and know who's involved. There are a lot of places to disappear on the ranch tonight. I'll get you somewhere safer tomorrow."

"Where?" The word was muffled in defeat as she covered her mouth with slim fingers.

"Adams's property tonight. Brian and I played there all the time. They won't think you're arrogant enough to hide right under their noses."

"Johnny." She gently took his arm before he could walk past her. "What happens if they find me?"

He sank into the bluest eyes he could remember. A face that he'd tried his best to let go. She'd never lied to him, always had faith in him. He was the one who'd turned his back on her, not trusting.

"Believe me, they won't. I know what I'm doing. I've hidden in a lot places worse than Aubrey, Texas. No one finds me when I dig in."

He reached for his cell, dialing the number Mabel had written on the notepad stuck to the fridge. "It's John. Change of plans—can you pack a bag and come stay with Dad overnight? Thanks."

"Brian called to warn me. Did he keep you out of the loop on purpose? No one knows you're here, do they?" Alicia asked once he'd hung up.

"That's our ace in the hole. They'll all be watching Brian and they think you're alone. I won't lie to you, Alicia. It's going to get rough, and plenty of people are going to say worse things than the accusations on television."

He glanced over his shoulder into the living room. His dad looked straight at him, smiling, and gave him a thumbs-up. If there had been doubts about leaving his dad to help Alicia before, there weren't any longer.

"I want my daughter back and I'm willing to do anything to make that happen. I trust you, Johnny."

"Good."

The real question was if he could trust himself.

Chapter Six

"Where's my mommy?" the kid asked for the hundredth time since she'd been hauled here kicking and screaming.

Tory had been sure they'd be caught before leaving Aubrey. But the dark windows and loud speakers of her ex's car had covered their escape and the kid's screaming. Then country back roads had hidden them again.

Lauren had cried until they'd convinced her of the lie. Part of the cover-up. Part of Patrick's brilliant plan. Part of their attempt to never be caught. Tell the kid her mother was testing her and would "rescue" her after they finished the game. It was no big deal. She could pretend she was on an adventure.

"Can't you make that kid shut up?" Her ex-boyfriend charged toward the little girl, but Tory stepped between them to calm him down. He turned and threw himself on the tattered cushions of the broken-down couch.

"What do you want me to do? You know if we hurt her we don't get paid." She should never have told Patrick that she'd help. And should have never have gone back to her ex to assist her pulling off this stupid plan. The bum always thought he was the boss, and he had the muscles to convince you. "Go back in the bedroom, honey, and play with your new toys."

"But can't I have a drink?" the kid asked. "When's this game going to be over?"

"Later, sweetheart." Tory scooted her inside the room and flipped the newly installed bolt to keep her there.

She passed too close and her ex's thick hand wrapped around her wrist. The same one he'd fractured last spring. It still hurt if she twisted it the wrong way and especially hurt when she tried to pull free. The bastard knew that. She'd yelped loud enough the first couple of times he'd grabbed her like this.

"The news thinks that kid's mother snatched her for the money."

"It's working just like I said it would," she agreed, hoping he'd let go before she cried from his tight grip.

"So I've been rethinkin' our arrangement. We can get more money. That idiot Weber is loaded."

"I'm not so sure. Seems kinda dicey." How would she explain this to Patrick?

"What can he do to us if we demand more? It's not like he can waltz to the police or his wife and tell them everything. This is a sure bet. We're in charge and he has to do what we say."

"I don't know if we should. My way seems like it's safer. We take the money and the mom takes the blame." She had to convince him to stay with the original agreement. She wasn't risking everything for half the pittance he thought they'd agreed to last week. She'd follow the plan, take all the money, leave this blustering jackass hanging and run off with Patrick.

"My way, we get lots more dough. I've seen them do this on TV lots of times."

He wanted to be in charge. How could she make it *his* plan? Her wrist was aching but she didn't pull away. She cozied up to the slime bucket, giving him full view of the extra cleavage in the tight shirt Patrick couldn't resist. "Don't they always get caught on TV?"

"Only if they leave DNA or somethin', and we're in the clear. That stupid Weber left his prints and gave us the bear to plant. We used gloves."

"But, honey." She tried to sound sweet in spite of the shooting pain in her arm. "You know I already took the ransom note you worked so hard on."

"We can make another."

Patrick had instructed them to let Lauren cut and glue the letters together. It had taken a long time, but only the kid's prints were on the paper. That one little thing had taken a four-year-old two solid mornings and afternoons to put together. Small pieces of paper needed to be thrown away and it had been her idea to leave them at Alicia's house. The scissors, magazines and scraps had been left on the kid's play table in Lauren's very own bedroom.

"Getting the kid to do it again will take a couple of more days," she said sweetly.

The lummox heaved her to his sweaty chest. Tory couldn't deny he had a great body. And wasn't bad to look at. That was why she'd been with him so long. If he could just control his mean streak and stop stinkin' like horses, she wouldn't mind getting together with him while she waited for all this to be over. He grabbed a handful of her hair and yanked backward. His hot breath landed between her breasts as she landed on his lap.

She knew what would come. She'd told Patrick, practically begged him to let her ask someone else. This was their best option, he'd explained. No one would look too closely if her ex moved back in, but they'd ask lots of questions if it was a stranger. Especially a stranger who moved in at the same time the kid disappeared.

So this way was smarter, and Patrick couldn't get mad if the inevitable happened. She'd let her ex have his way. Keep him happy and hopefully get him to forget about changing the plan. With any luck, he wouldn't knock her around too much in the process.

Tory bit her lip and held her breath, preparing herself. Three more days and she'd be flying first-class to Paris with Patrick. Her imagination drifted, picturing another lover, more skilled, gentler. She fell backward, dropping to the floor when suddenly released.

"What did I do?"

"You don't ever do nothin'." He shoved off the couch, kicking out with his boot.

Tory saw the red-faced rage burst from her partner and covered her face, prepared for the mean left punch she'd received many, many times. It didn't come. She timidly stood, uncertain what would happen. She'd never seen him like this. A backhand to the side of her cheek spun her across the arm of the couch.

"Get out of here before I really show you what I think," he bellowed.

Tory ran to the kid's door, twisted the bolt and darted inside. She'd been frightened of the jerk before, but never like this. That anger she'd seen ripped into his heart—if he still had one.

The bastard who exploded wasn't her ex-boyfriend. He was worse. She didn't know what he'd become or what drugs he was doing now, but he'd turned into an angry striking machine.

She shrank to the floor, leaning against the thin

wall, her mind whirling with ways to get out of this mess. She couldn't go back out there and pretend to like that monster.

Three more days. Could she do this for even one? For Paris? For Patrick? She could do it for him. She would do it for a million dollars. But now she had to come up with a story about her face. She was certain it would be black-and-blue when she went to work the next day. She needed to pretend everything was normal and not give the police any reason to question her.

A cool little hand soothed her hot cheek. "Are you okay, Tory? Your face is sunburned."

"Yeah. Just a little scared. I'm going to sleep in here tonight."

"Are you scared of the big man, too? He yells loud like Grandma Weber." Her small four-year-old hand covered her mouth. "Oops. She yells more when I call her Grandma."

Lauren's embarrassed giggle was sweet, but not enough to make Tory forget who'd just hit her into the next county.

Nothing in the room would slide in front of the door. Nothing to use for protection. Just a mattress on the floor and plastic blocks in the corner. Tory heard determined footsteps heading their direction. She braced herself against the thin door.

Silence.

Click.

The bastard had locked her in with their prisoner, and her cell was in her purse in the kitchen.

"I'll take care of the money arrangements, Tory. You manage the runt," he shouted through the wood. "And you ain't going to work no more. I ain't no babysitter."

She allowed Lauren to crawl in her lap, hugging the little girl close. This wasn't the plan.

Lauren tugged on Tory's shirtfront to get her attention. "How long is Mommy going to be gone? I don't like it here."

"Me neither, sweetie. Me neither."

Chapter Seven

The dilapidated barn stall still held the smell of manure after years of nonuse. Alicia was hot, sticky and had no intention of lying under the cover of the sleeping bag, until Johnny reminded her rat snakes loved barns. The horrible creatures could actually climb into the rafters and wait. So, of course, she couldn't close her eyes and was stuck searching the decaying wooden beams.

"You just had to mention snakes," she complained, hearing him actually laugh.

"You ever going to sleep?"

She noticed the flick of an LED watch from his direction.

"What time is it?"

"Twenty-three minutes after the last time you asked," he mumbled.

He sounded muffled, maybe facedown with his mouth pushed into his muscles. Johnny wasn't worried about the nasty snakes that bit when they were provoked. He'd never been afraid and had constantly irritated the cold-blooded things when they were younger.

"Are you sure we can't sleep outside? It's sweltering in here." She tossed the bag off her, keeping the zippered end only over her bare feet. "There's absolutely no breeze."

"I was only teasing about the snakes, you know." His clear, rich voice came from slightly higher, like he was raised on his elbows.

He was bare chested, just like he'd been when she'd arrived at the Double Bar earlier that afternoon. The memory of his sculpted muscles sent her thoughts in a wild direction. She chased her thoughts back to slithering, long things hanging above her.

Snakes were a safer subject to concentrate on. The cold eating machines weren't nearly as likeable as a man who had promised to find Lauren.

"The thought of snakes isn't really what's bothering me. I'm letting my mind fixate on it so I don't think about other things." *Lots of other things*.

"Like?" he asked, sounding resigned they were talking in the dark instead of sleeping.

"Lauren's been gone less than a week and I feel so alone. Every part of me aches."

"I'd be worried if it didn't. You've taken an emotional beating. Hurting's a lot better than feeling nothing at all," he said softly.

"Is that what you feel? Nothing?"

"Me? Negative. I'm confused more than anything."

She heard the slick of the nylon rustling, gave up and looked at him. The crescent moon still spilled enough light to see a few old wounds on his shoulder. He sat, one arm wrapped around a knee that he'd brought close to his chest.

"Confused? I don't understand. You were very decisive ordering me what to pack and what to do. I witnessed exactly what your dad is always telling me. How you're such an in-charge leader and all."

"My dad?" He drew his brows together, a permanent crease between them now that hadn't been there in his teens.

"Yeah. I mean, he'd tell me before the stroke."

He stretched his back by raising his arms above his head.

Goodness, he had muscles on top of muscle. There couldn't be an inch of fat on him anywhere. She couldn't watch and looked out the door to the star-studded sky.

"Did you spend a lot of time with Dad?" he asked, settling back against the stall post.

She sat, leaning on the wall opposite him. "Sure. J.W. and Brian checked on me after Dwayne's dad died and I was alone with Lauren."

"I didn't know."

"There are a lot of things you don't know."

"I get the picture. I missed quite a bit around here. Hey, we should get some shut-eye. It might be the last sound sleep we get for a while."

"I don't think I can sleep. There's just too much going on in here." She pointed a finger to her head. "The thoughts are so random. Mixed with a desire to be held. When we hugged out on the drive, I realized just how long it had been since I've been in a man's arms."

"Alicia."

"But the guilt mixed throughout all those thoughts makes me want to cry. Lauren's gone and…and…there's nobody. I can't do this alone." She covered her face with her hands, drawing her knees to her body, suddenly chilled at the prospect of never seeing her daughter again.

"Alicia. Come here."

John gently tugged her hands into his. He'd moved next to her and wrapped her in his arms, kissing the top of her head as it dropped to his chest. His gentleness warmed her heart. He smoothed her hair and she felt his breath close to her ear.

"Go ahead and cry, just let it go. I've got your six."

THE WOMAN IN his arms had cried herself to sleep. She'd forgotten about snakes, only to replace one worry with several more—fright, attraction, the unknown. Fatigue had finally claimed her around two in the morning. Earlier, he could have been out like a flipped switch. His life in the navy had taught him the importance of sleeping upon command.

So why couldn't he sleep?

He was wound tighter than a coil of wire, that's why. Alicia was more than just a beautiful girl who needed help changing a tire. He was her *only* chance at finding her daughter. Not to mention freeing his brother.

If his guess was correct, he was the only chance she had at staying alive. It was logical that her enemies wouldn't want her around to continue fighting them. If caught, she'd conveniently meet with a fatal accident or suicide, leaving behind a note clearing the Webers. Telling her about the danger wasn't a current option, but he'd need to sooner or later.

A plan of action was what they needed. Maybe that was what his brain had been searching for before it could rest. What did he have to work with?

Weapons. Just the revolver his dad owned.

Stealth. One thing on their side was that no one knew he was in town. He hadn't shared with the police department he'd been headed home. Alicia had commented that her friends thought they'd seen Brian drive through town. They could assume Alicia had an accomplice, but they wouldn't know who. And Mabel had sworn herself to secrecy without being asked.

Communication. He could call his team for information. No one would be monitoring his cell. No. He couldn't involve the team. He was the lieutenant who'd come up through the ranks. Not only an officer, but a friend. They'd feel obligated to help. This op had to stay off book and had dire consequences if he was caught. It was the end of his career.

Alicia shifted and he let her slide down his ribs, cradling her head in the crook of his arm until she rested on his lap. It was still warm in the barn, but he draped his sleeping bag over her legs anyway. She turned her head and shifted to her side, drawing her hands under her chin.

He could remember another night they'd spent under the stars. Having fallen asleep at the lake, they woke up with the sun and tried to sneak back to their respective homes. Man, oh, man. They'd received a tongue-lashing up one side and down the other from his mom. It was all about how they needed to be responsible. And what if anyone else had seen them?

His mother's voice was in his head as clear as if she were standing in front of him. *You've got to take care of the ones you love, Joy-o.* How many times had she said that? Boy-o and Joy-o, her nicknames for them. *B* for Brian and *J* for John.

How quickly he'd forgotten. Put out of his thoughts to avoid the hurt as soon as she'd been gone.

Was that what Alicia wanted to do? No. She cared too much. But why was she facing this on her own? Where were her brother and dad? What had happened to their property?

More questions that somehow he knew would cause her pain if asked. He couldn't do that yet.

Alicia was family, according to his mom. She had been since the first time she'd come over for cookies. He hooked her long waves around her ear and stared at her nose, at the freckles that had been there as long as he'd known her. *Is she worth losing your career?*

"Absolutely."

His whisper caused Alicia to stir again. He gently placed her head on the sleeping bag and eased away. If he was going to be awake, he might as well make good use of the time. Pulling his phone from his pack, he walked into the field.

He'd debated since leaving the ranch whether to call for assistance. He knew his limitations. There was no doubt he could protect Alicia. And he would find her daughter. But finding the proof to clear his brother of the accusations meant finding the proof that would convict the actual kidnappers.

He owed Brian after everything he'd sacrificed. He'd been mad all this time, and for what? He dialed a number on his way from the barn, walking toward a familiar tree where he, his brother and Dwayne had attempted to build a tree house.

Devlin McClain picked up on the fourth ring. "This had better be good, Sloane. Do you know what time it is?"

"I've got a problem, Dev."

"What's her name?" His bunkmate laughed.

"Cut the crap. Do you know any former SEALs or specialists in Texas?"

"Texas?" His response sounded much more alert. "Just what kind of trouble are you in?"

"Maybe somebody gone private security? I need some quiet research and fieldwork."

"I think I can find someone. Seriously, you going to tell me what's up? Don't pull that 'it's better if you don't know' stuff."

"A friend's little girl has been kidnapped."

"Runaway dad? You want me to do a search—"

"No. It's about the money. I think the kid's close by. Alicia's being set up to take the fall."

John heard a string of words on the other end and couldn't agree more. "I hate it when they use kids."

"I can't take any risks with this one, Dev. Nothing with the team, but I need someone to check out the possible suspects. Someone willing to bend the law a bit."

"And if you don't get anywhere? You know who

to call?" Dev declared, he didn't ask or suggest. "With you gone, the team's been given leave."

"I can't ask that, man."

"How many times you save my hide, John? Anything you need, you've got it."

"Thanks."

"I'll have someone contact you ASAP. This number secure?"

"Should be. I'll call if I switch."

"You should hear from me in a couple of hours. You got someone watching your back?"

"This can go south all sorts of ways. Stay clear. You hearing me?" He hoped his friend took his words seriously. A team of SEALs loose in the area wouldn't be easy to hide.

"How's your dad and, um…you see your brother yet?"

Dev was the only person he'd shared a split second of concern with regarding coming home. "Dad's going to make it. The stroke left him slightly paralyzed and unable to talk."

"That's tough, man."

"Yeah. It's also something I can't talk about. I need my battery."

"Right. Two hours and you'll hear from me with a time and place to meet locally."

"There's a lake nearby. Just tell me when. And thanks, Dev."

He powered down the cell and stuck it in his

back pocket. There was no way he'd be attempting to sleep now. He looked up in the tree, saw an old board still secure at one end and rusty nails on the other. He pulled himself up and yanked, jerking it free.

He could see the entire field from the lower branches. It looked the same as it had the summers he'd played there, with a major exception. No horses. This place used to be full of them.

"John?" Alicia called from the barn door.

"Right here." He swung down and jogged the fifty yards or so back.

"What were you doing up in the tree?"

"Grabbing this." He tucked the board in a safe place inside the half-rotten door. "Where are the horses? Have things gotten so hard around here they were shutting down the horse farm and selling the stock?"

"Shauna sold it off."

"Dwayne's grandfather must be turning in his grave." He wanted to tilt her head back to look at him, but he was afraid to touch her. She was vulnerable and attractive, and he knew exactly what he wanted to do. It was not what she *needed* him to do. "Why are you awake?"

"Same to you. Why are you awake?"

"SEALs rarely get eight hours of shut-eye."

"Neither do mothers."

The teasing in her eyes was gone. A look of

hopelessness filled her eyes with tears again. She was thinking about Lauren.

"These probably seem like empty words to you, Alicia. But you've got to be strong. All the time. Never let your guard down and let the emotion get the better of you. If you do…they win."

"Right." She pressed her lips together and joined him leaning on the decaying wood. "What do we do now?"

"That is a very good question."

Chapter Eight

"Are you sure this is the best of plans? I'd rather be looking for Lauren." Alicia had mentioned that fact in every other sentence, and John had seemed to ignore her. "Maybe we could be doing anything other than illegally entering a house I lived in for a short time."

She'd gladly stay in the sun waiting. It was much better than heading inside.

"Each visit to this house reminds me of how Shauna manipulated Roy into getting married. Visiting after that was horrible. The first Christmas Dwayne and I were here was excruciating. We were forced to listen to Roy compare Dwayne's mother to every decision Shauna made. I actually felt sorry for her at one point. But I'm still uncertain this is the best way to use our time."

"I've got a former U.S. Marines specialist looking into the Webers. We're meeting him at fifteen hundred. He'll locate every property. Pull their phone and bank records, their emails. We're going to find Lauren. Trust me."

"Then what are we doing here?"

"It's reconnaissance. I need to familiarize myself with the lay of the land again. Maybe find a safe place for you to lay low." He put a pair of binoculars back to his eyes.

"I told you that the Adams farm is for sale. Shauna lives in Frisco now. The horses are ready to be auctioned tomorrow. She emptied the house of anything worth money and promptly called a local Realtor. It's still listed, but can't be sold, much to that witch's frustration. The house may belong to Shauna, but the land around it belongs to Lauren."

"Then why are there three cars here?"

"It's probably the cleaning staff." Alicia knew one was her father-in-law's. He'd left the classic to her, but it was caught in probate court. It deserved better care, but she couldn't afford to professionally store it in the garage. Shauna's lawsuit prevented her from touching it at all.

She was with John at the edge of the yard, having hiked from the old barn where they'd stayed the night. With no stables to run and no one living in the house, it may have been the safest place for them to hide after all.

They had enough food for a couple of days, and they weren't in the wilderness by any means. John had grabbed a fishing pole. Hiding wasn't the problem. He'd convinced her to come with him because they'd be searching for Lauren. But they weren't.

"What do you expect to find?"

"Man, Alicia. Just trust me. This is what I do."

"I have to take your word that you're good at what you do, John Sloane. But you don't have carte blanche over my life. I appreciate everything. Just remember that it's my little girl who's missing. I'm a little bit anxious, especially since the police think *I'm* responsible somehow."

She hadn't intended to huff when she crossed her arms. But she had. She wanted to sound slightly indignant and was afraid she'd sounded spoiled instead.

"I apologize. I'm not used to people questioning my orders."

"This is a joint effort," she reminded him.

"Right." He placed the binoculars to his eyes, letting the one word sound like three or four syllables as it slipped through his lips.

It was far from being a joint effort. She didn't miss the sarcasm.

"There's only one person moving around. A young woman. Got any idea who she is?"

She adjusted the binoculars and saw a short blonde wearing jeans and a T-shirt. "That's probably Andra's Angels. I recognize the swirly *A*s on her shirt. It's a cleaning service."

"It looks like she's packing up. We'll wait down by the gulch."

With each ray of sun poking through the cooler shade, she could feel her skin baking and her temper boiling. She wanted to *do* something. Be proactive. Not sit around and wait at a dried-up creek bed.

"While we're waiting, you can explain more about your plan and why it's so dang important to hide."

"All right. Here are the facts. You're being framed—along with Brian—for the kidnapping of your daughter. Once they take you to jail, they'll probably insist you go to Denton County, where you'll be involved in a fatal fight or feel such remorse you'll commit suicide."

Totally deflated, she plopped on the hard ground next to him. He sounded so matter-of-fact recounting his supposition. He'd clearly thought through the options and jumped to a dismal end. "And with me gone, they get control over Lauren's trust. To get Lauren back, I'd sign over the trust fund this minute and walk away forever. Don't they know that?"

"They don't. Whoever they are, they don't think that way. They believe everyone desires money as much as they do. Just remember, we're assuming it's Shauna and Patrick, but right now, everyone's a suspect."

"How do you plan on finding my daughter?"

"There are a lot of variables they need to control. Since the police have been watching them, other people must be involved and doing the dirty work. There must be details somewhere. We'll find their trail, but we have to keep you alive along the way." He set the binoculars to his side and patted her knee. "Don't worry, I'm actually good at this."

He looked concerned, but didn't smile to reassure her. Not a grin noting confidence that he knew all the answers, not even a slow tilt of his lips showing comfort. Come to think about it, he hadn't grinned since they'd been in the driveway together that first day and he'd seen her. Had she? She couldn't smile with Lauren gone.

"What happened to you, Johnny?"

"It's been twelve years, Alicia."

"You've changed. You're so serious and realistic. You're certainly not pulling any punches."

"Do you want me to sugarcoat the reality of the situation?"

"No. I… I've been sugarcoating much too much of my life as it is. I want Lauren back and I'm willing to do anything and every—"

"Shh." His finger went unerringly to her lips as his eyes searched behind her. "Someone's coming."

"What do we do?" she asked in a panicked whisper.

His strong arm dropped around her shoulders and in an instant her back was on the ground. Her head was in the bend of John's arm, bringing his body on top of her. For a split second she thought he was just protecting her, but then he grinned. A teasing gleam from their teenage years reached his eyes as his lips captured hers.

"Stop being shocked and pretend to kiss me," he whispered against her lips. He slid a knee between her legs, supporting himself so she could breathe, but leaving no breath of space separating them.

It wasn't shock at kissing him that she was experiencing. It was a shock at realizing twelve years could pass and desire for this man could rush back so fully.

Even after loving Dwayne. This was different. She wanted to feel, to be held, to be desired. It was like capturing a stolen moment from her youth.

She parted her lips, hungry for the contact. His tongue danced with hers. She slid her hands around his back, wanting to lift his shirt and feel the contours of the muscles she'd seen last night. The familiar feel of a strong body protecting her from the world was a heady sensation.

Footsteps crunched sticks and dried leaves that fell from the elm trees earlier that spring. John's body tightened becoming more rigid, more alert.

"Oh, I beg your pardon," a somewhat familiar older voice said.

"Mr. Searcy?" John asked, breaking their contact and lifting his chest from hers.

"Brian, boy. I didn't recognize you with that head of hair gone. Looks good. Is that you, Miss Alicia?"

Joe Searcy had worked for the Adams family all of their lives. She'd witnessed him breaking up many fights between the boys and escorting them to their parents more than once by holding their ears.

Alicia shoved at John's pectorals and scrambled to a sitting position, straightening her tank top. All the while both men chuckled.

"It's about time you two got together," Joe said with his cigarette-battered vocal cords. "I remember catching you around the property a time or two."

"That was John, Mr. Searcy." John laced his fingers through hers and smiled goofily while pretending to be his twin. Pretending unsuccessfully. Brian was never goofy.

"You're really reminding him of that?" she whispered, knowing Joe was hard of hearing.

How anyone ever got them confused was beyond her. That goofy mischievousness was 100 percent John.

"What's that?" the older man complained. "And, Brian, why so formal? You've been calling me Joe since you've been stopping by to help around the place for Miss Alicia."

"Yes, sir," John said.

"Sorry I mumbled, Joe. It's good to see you outside, but where's your walking stick?" She disengaged from John, stood and brushed the dirt from her jeans. "John, would you—" She stopped herself, remembering at the last minute he was pretending to be his brother. "John would get so embarrassed when you caught us. Remember?"

She went to Joe and gave him a hug. John stood and hunted for a stick, quick to understand what she'd been about to ask him.

"Miss Alicia, I don't need a walking stick."

"Now, Joe, we agreed after the fall you took last March that you'd get a walking stick for uneven ground. It's either that or a cane. You promised."

"Always looking out for everybody. How long you two been seeing each other?"

She shook her head at John, warning him not to answer. He handed Joe a sturdy-looking stick, smooth enough for his callused but weaker hand to grip.

"Thank you, Boy-o. I forgot the one you brought by the house. No need to make another. And I'll remember to use it. Now, you two should think about finding a cooler place to cuddle. Why, out here, you could have a sunstroke getting all hot and bothered." Joe waggled his bushy eyebrows at them.

Heaven help me.

Certain she'd changed several shades of embarrassing pink in a few seconds, she watched John smile and nod in agreement. She attempted to dart her eyes and jerk her head away from Joe to indicate she was ready to escape. John didn't seem interested or just flat-out ignored her. He seemed to be having a good laugh at her expense.

"How's your father, Brian?"

"Better, sir. Thanks for asking. Alicia's taking great care of him. In fact, he's the one who suggested we take a break today."

"Good. Good. He up for visitors yet?" Joe finally took a step away.

"Probably do him good to see you, sir." John helped the old man up the slight incline.

"I'll plan on it. Bye now, I'm off to lunch."

"Oh, Joe. Would you mind keeping this a secret?" She pointed to John and herself. "We'd like to keep it quiet awhile."

"Mum's the word, Miss Alicia. You should try that old storage barn on the Kruegerville acreage for some privacy. You might have to saddle a ride, but no one goes there since Mr. Adams… passed." He leaned on the stick and took several steps. "Mum's the word."

John stood next to her as an icon from their youth meandered back the way he'd come.

"That brought back some memories," John said, scratching his head. "I don't get it. He didn't ask about Lauren, but he knew about Dad."

"I told him about J.W. He refuses to have cataract

surgery, and his vision is blurry. So he doesn't read the paper or watch television anymore."

"Was he talking about the barn we had that haunted house in one year? That thing still standing?"

"I guess so. I had no idea Roy went there. He never mentioned it to me."

"That should go on our list of things to check out."

John turned away from her and jogged back to get the binoculars he'd set on the ground. She had no clue if he meant to check out the barn for potential information or to use it as Joe had suggested.

But she knew that her first thought leaned heavily toward the latter. And that both frightened and excited her at the possibility John's thoughts had gone there, too.

Chapter Nine

The short visit with Mr. Searcy hadn't brought up too many memories of getting caught in their youth. John was still thinking about the kiss in the gully today. It took top-notch self-discipline and concentration to stay sane enough to continue looking for the approaching threat. How had she gotten to be a better kisser? And man, if they hadn't cooled their heels over the past fifteen minutes in the presence of the old man, he might have thrown her onto her back—kissing her into oblivion again.

"Joe will probably mention seeing me at the lunch counter today. He's there every Monday and Friday and bound to hear about Lauren. We can only pray that he doesn't mention seeing you."

"Yeah, pray." He didn't really expect fate or luck to be working on their side. "I'll lose my anonymity as soon as Joe has lunch if Mabel doesn't get Brian out of jail."

"Are we heading to the house?" Alicia asked.

"Affirmative."

They walked into the bright noon July heat, across a field as dry as fire tinder. *What had happened to everything?*

"Say *affirmative* around other people and they'll know you're not Brian for sure. Of course, I still don't know how anyone could get the two of you confused."

"The hard thing to believe is that you don't. How?"

"How what?"

"How do you tell us apart? Besides the obvious haircut."

She shrugged. He stopped them at the backyard to verify the maid had left. One car now. The other must have been Joe's. He hopped the wooden fence and waited for Alicia to climb.

"Show-off. What are we looking for once we're inside?"

"I don't know. Let's find an entrance and then think about it." He tried a couple of windows. All locked. He was about to put his elbow through the glass on the back door when Alicia pulled it to a stop.

"Why don't we just use this?" She dangled a lone key at the end of her tanned arm.

"You could have said something."

"And where's the fun in that?" She slipped the key in the dead bolt and a second time in the knob. "I warned you that the place has changed a lot."

"Yeah, it's empty. What happened to everything?" He shut the door and had to flip on the light to see.

More than just furniture was missing. There weren't any mementos, knickknacks, family pictures…nothing. Objects that had been there the entire time they'd grown up. Dwayne had lost his mother at a very young age. His grandparents had moved back in and had no reason to change things around. His dad had told them more than once that he liked keeping his wife's belongings close to their everyday life.

Alicia gave him a look and he knew the answer. Roy had married Shauna and she'd changed the open kitchen area into a dark cave. Heavy drapery blocked the sunlight.

"She didn't like seeing the barn and constantly complained about how her eyes hurt in the sun."

"Was she hungover or high?"

"That would have been understandable. I don't think so. Honestly, I have no idea." Alicia's voice sounded older, sadder.

More than the room was dark. Gone was the tenderness this woman had shown for Joe Searcy. She walked through the house with her arms crossed and hands tucked into fists.

"A lot of things were packed away as soon as she moved in. She told the movers to donate it someplace. Roy had it stored somewhere for Dwayne to look through one day. Less than a year later he was gone. Roy followed not too long after."

She squeezed her eyes shut and he patted her shoulder, afraid of the thoughts passing through his head. Inappropriate thoughts of desire shot through his body and made him drop his hand.

"The court said she could sell anything that they'd bought as a couple."

"There's not much left." He gestured to the near-empty everything. "I know it's difficult, but I've got to ask. Why did Roy marry someone young enough to be his daughter? Was he that lonely?"

"She went through a divorce just after Dwayne and I married. I talked to her one day at the grocery store. Then she asked to come over. And kept asking. We didn't want to be rude and I actually thought she was lonely. She must have come over when Roy was alone one night. I think she tricked him into thinking she may be pregnant. He never said anything to anyone. Especially not Dwayne."

"Is there a wall safe?"

"No, I don't think so. And even if there was, he never kept anything here. All his papers were in his office at the show stables. I told you earlier you wouldn't find anything." Her voice choked up a little and he could see tears flooding her eyes.

"Sorry for putting you through this. I didn't mean to upset you more." *Don't touch her, man.* He didn't listen to himself. Pulling her into his arms and letting her cry was probably the worst idea he'd ever had. Right up there with that failed maneuver in Afghanistan.

A bad idea, because he couldn't trust himself. He wanted a second kiss and more. They were both adults. They could handle a real relationship now. He rested his chin on her head and encouraged her cheek to lie against his chest. Wisps of her curls caressed his hot skin. Hard to believe less than a week ago he'd been halfway around the world in mock maneuvers.

What the hell was he doing?

Waiting here was putting her in danger. Bringing her inside with him put her in danger. They should have been in and out. Fast. And he was delaying so he could hold an old girlfriend.

Emotion had no place in reconnaissance and was not allowed in rescues. Period. There was no room in his lifestyle and career for emotional attachments. He'd seen too many of his buddies lose their families. Partial custody or not seeing their kids for months at a time tore them up and made them lose their edge.

Man, she has a little girl. Dwayne's kid. He couldn't do this.

"If you're okay, let's get out of here." He held her shoulders and kept looking over the top of her head, to keep from seeing the sadness in her eyes.

Sadness for another man she loved—even if he was gone.

"I'm fine."

Words with no substance, if wiping away tears was an indicator. And yet she stood straight and didn't complain.

Was it strength? Completely different from what he experienced with his team. A kind that he hadn't seen in a long time. Not since his mom died and the community had rallied around his family.

Alicia should come with warning signs. Emotional ties were dangerous ground for a SEAL who traversed the globe and never knew if he'd return. He needed to build a wall too high for her to climb. He never surrendered. Never would.

A car door shut and he jerked to a stop. Alicia froze. He didn't have to tell her to be quiet or to remain calm. She was. He saw it in her questioning expression. He pointed upstairs. She turned, pulled her shoes off like they had each time they'd snuck up those same stairs as teenagers and soundlessly left him.

About to follow, he turned off the lights and from the corner of his eye spotted the key Alicia had left on the counter. *Damn.* He had training on his side and nothing else. Moving quickly, he swept the key into his pocket and turned the bolt. Good thing the drapes were heavy and no one outside could see shadows.

He peered through the minuscule view available at the window and saw two policemen—one older and one younger. They were both looking in the flowerpots.

"I'll find the key," the experienced officer said. "Go keep a watch out front to see if anyone leaves."

"It's hot out here. She's long gone, sir. Everyone knows she took off to San Antonio and left Sloane to take the rap. Let the Texas Rangers locate her. Coming here doesn't make sense."

"Randall, I swear, if you backtalk me one more time today, you'll be looking for a new job. She left her keys in the car, son. The keys to the houses were missing. Use your noggin."

The older officer was smarter than John had given him credit for. And Alicia hadn't followed his instructions. The patrolman, a kid he didn't recognize, reluctantly shuffled his feet around front. They couldn't get out of the house without being seen.

Fighting the kid out front wasn't an option. If he didn't know him, the kid knew what Brian looked like and that he was in jail. Assuming it was John he'd fought wouldn't be a giant leap for anyone. He hated hiding, but he couldn't risk the police announcing that he was back in town.

He got upstairs, heard the door in the kitchen creak open. Where was she? Dwayne's room was empty. He felt the wave of heat. Window? It was open a crack. They couldn't get to the ground without being seen, but they could hide in the tree next to the house. Alicia could think on her feet. Good to know.

The climb up the giant oak took little effort on his part. He'd shut the window behind him and caught sight of Alicia as high up as the tree would support her weight. She sat in the V of a branch, lacing her shoes.

He got far away from the window and the woman he was trying to protect. If they looked out and spotted him, they might miss Alicia. All they needed was a little luck and for him to screw his head on straight. *Start thinking, man.*

Searching the house didn't take long for the chief. They hadn't disturbed anything—there was nothing to mess with. No one could tell they'd been there. The two men grumbled as they got in the squad car and drove off.

He waited a full five minutes, checking his watch every thirty seconds, before he climbed down to the ground. Alicia followed.

Silently, they proceeded across the open field, choosing the shortest distance they'd be exposed. They hit the far tree line with a barbed-wire fence and followed it just as quickly down to the gully.

When they stopped, Alicia was bent at the waist and gulping air. He was used to running in the heat and could make it to the old barn where their gear was stashed.

"Wait here and catch your breath. I'll get the binoculars. Then we need to clear out of the barn before they check all the property again."

"Sure." She sat.

It wasn't long before he saw her lie on the ground.

"Why do you think they were looking at the house?" she asked when he returned. "Do you think Joe told the guys at lunch?"

"The key."

"Shoot. I'm so sorry—I didn't think they'd notice. I'll listen to you from now on. Promise."

"Time to get moving." He'd given her time to catch her breath, and neither of the police officers had doubled back. He'd been careless enough with her safety today.

From this point forward, he'd treat her as he would any other civilian he was ordered to escort to safety. No more distractions. No more emotion. No more holding. And definitely no more kissing.

Chapter Ten

SEAL versus SEAL. There had been nothing but an overabundance of testosterone since John had met his contact. The man obviously wasn't the stranger who John had earlier explained they'd be meeting at the lake. They clearly knew each other, and John was furious.

"Nice to see you, too," the young man said as John grabbed the younger man's shirtfront.

John released him, but neither man backed away. "What are you doing here? I told you not to come."

If either of the men puffed out their chests again, she would push them both in the water to cool off. She watched, sitting at the end of the walk where she'd been tempted to pull her shoes off and dip her feet in the lake. Right until John reminded her they might have to climb another tree—referring to their narrow escape from the police chief.

"You need my help," the stranger shouted, staying nose to nose.

Good thing they'd rendezvoused on a deserted

boat dock on Lake Ray Roberts. If she hadn't been worried about being discovered, their classic posturing might even be comical.

"I asked for a favor, Dev. You weren't supposed to hitch a ride with a pilot and bring the gear personally," John answered tersely. "You said you understood that."

So his name was Dev, and her assumption about him being part of John's unit was correct. They were similar in height and haircut, but nothing else except perhaps some navy SEAL arm muscles.

The water looked very inviting. Jeans weren't the best thing to be wearing in this heat, and being this near the water made her sticky from the humidity. But it was nothing compared to the images that kept playing through her head of where her daughter might be. She wanted her back.

These two needed to do more and argue less. Or not at all.

"The equipment stays with me. It's my personal gear. I'm here and that's the end of it."

"Excuse me." She hesitantly approached them, attempting to interrupt. Both men ignored her. "John? Dev?"

Two sets of SEAL jaws were visibly clenched in determination. Neither one seemed about to flinch. John's hands were fisted. Dev's legs were braced to take a shove or a punch. She had to stop this before it came to blows and someone reported them to the police.

"I thought you guys were friends," she said, laying a hand on John's arm.

He turned toward her so fast that she jerked backward. Her feet tangled under her and sent her flying. She watched John's eyes grow large and his mouth open. He said something as she fell. She was grimacing at the punishment her bottom would endure when she hit that solid wood, so she couldn't comprehend his words.

She kept falling. No wooden dock. She was headed for the water. She inhaled deeply, but too late. The splash caught her at the same time her mouth was open and she sucked lake water. She kicked hard, ready for air, and popped her head above water.

Coughing, sputtering, floundering.

"You okay, Alicia?" John asked.

Hands grabbed her shirt and hauled her to sit on the edge. Strong hands patted her back. Her hair was plastered to her face, so she couldn't see. Her wet shoes tugged at her legs with their weight.

"You okay, sweetheart?" Comforting hands were at her elbow, trying to help her stand.

She twisted some of the water from her hair and began to smile at the endearment. Wait. *That* voice, sounding so Texas, was the *other* SEAL.

"Back off, Dev." John sounded just as angry as before.

"I was just asking." Dev's hands held firm.

"Shut up. The both of—" cough "—you just shut up." She cleared her throat. "Or I'll send you into the water—" cough "—to cool down." She managed to raise her croaky voice a little and slapped the boards on either side of her for emphasis. Then she coughed a couple of times and cleared more water from her lungs, losing all the emphasis she'd gained.

It took a minute, and they patiently tapped her back until she thought she'd be black-and-blue. "This is ridiculous. Back off and don't touch me."

Both men stood, took a couple of steps in opposite directions and were silent. Blessedly silent.

She took her time arranging her hair where it belonged behind her head. She wiped the lake droplets off her face and arms. She toed off her shoes and ignored the warning look from John. It would take forever for her shoes to completely dry, especially if her feet were in them. It was enough that she'd be miserable in the wet denim and underwear.

On the bright side, she was much cooler and no longer sticky.

"Now, boys," she said sweetly as if she were talking to six-year-olds. She braided her hair before it dried in a wild frizzy mess. They both turned, standing similarly. "How sweet. You're both at attention."

John immediately relaxed. Dev stood more like he was at morning roll call or something. She crossed to John's friend, who had come to rescue her daughter, and extended her hand.

"I'm Alicia Adams, and I can't tell you how much it means to us that you've come to help. Thanks just doesn't seem enough."

"My pleasure, ma'am. Lieutenant Devlin McClain. Sloane and I are on the same team."

"And obviously friends. Thank you."

Then she turned to John, shooting him a forceful look with every indication he should also thank this man who had come to help, putting everything on the line for them.

"Thanks," he said, looking to the water at the last minute.

At least he'd gotten the message. She clapped her hands together. "Okay, then. Here's how it's going to be."

"Actually, I think I should take it from here," John said.

"I rented a cabin and I have the gear. Maybe I should tell you what I've discovered." Dev didn't flinch or break eye contact with his teammate.

"No more arguing," she warned, pointing fingers at them both. "Lauren's been missing five days.

Time's running out. She's scared, and who knows what else has happened."

All the sturdy walls she'd built to hold the trouble at bay started dissolving. The tears threatened. Then filled her eyes. Her throat tightened, this time from emotion. She pressed her palms against her eyes to prevent the meltdown.

It didn't work. John's arms engulfed her. She recognized his comforting stroke on her hair and hated that a simple hug from him could make her feel better. She had no right to feel better while Lauren was gone.

"We'll find your daughter, ma'am."

"Dev, what we're doing is illegal." John spoke over the top of her head. "If you get caught, it's a court martial—dishonorable discharge if we're lucky. Maybe military prison."

"Then let's not get caught," Dev replied matter-of-factly.

John sort of growled. She felt it under her hands. He cared so strongly for those around him. How could he have turned from his brother twelve years ago and never thought twice about any of them again?

She sniffed and backed away. John's T-shirt was wet with an imprint of her body. "We need his help. I certainly can't break down a door or overpower those men who tied me up. Please, Johnny. I have to find her."

She pleaded with him. She'd beg again if that was what it took. She desperately needed to hold her baby. They'd lost so much and were so alone. She was all Lauren could remember. Her little girl had to be scared to death.

"WE SHOULDN'T HAVE left her all alone," Tory complained, hoping her ex would turn the horrible truck he'd stolen around and forget this wild demand for more money.

"The brat was happy with the new toy. If you're all worried, then remember to be quick about this and not screw around."

"I hope nothing happens to her. She could choke on that dry sandwich we gave her or something else. Then what would we do?"

"Same thing we're doing now, collect a million dollars and give them the kid."

She saw something in his eyes that hadn't been there before. He wasn't just angry, he might actually kill Lauren. God, she didn't want to go to jail for murdering a kid or anybody. "You're sure it's a good idea to ask for more money?"

"They're going to pay." He hit the steering wheel with his thick fists. "Every rich son of a bitch that's screwed me is going to pay through this guy."

She wondered which rich men he was talking about. He'd never had anything worth taking from him, but she didn't want to rile him more. They were minutes away from delivering the second ransom note, which Patrick knew nothing about.

All hell was about to break loose.

It had been his idea to become real kidnappers instead of remaining the hired help. All her plans for Paris seemed further away than ever before. She recognized the Frisco side street. "You want me to walk three blocks to get to the Weber house?"

"Get goin'. You look stupid with that wig. No one will recognize you, so stop being so scared."

His crazy idea for walking down the street with a stroller might just work. She already had a long dark wig, big sunglasses that covered half her face and boots. She'd sweated through the tight-fitting shirt, but she wasn't trying to impress anyone.

"Don't forget this." He threw a huge straw hat they'd gotten at the Dollar Mart across the cab.

She shut the door, grabbed the stroller they'd found in a truck bed and put a sack of trash under a blanket. She fluffed it around until it looked close enough to a fake baby.

It crossed her mind to run as she took off quickly down the sidewalk to round the block. She could knock on someone's door and ask for help. Tory Preston could be the hero, tell the police where Lauren Adams was being held and watch her brutal ex be placed safely behind bars. Then he'd tell the cops all about how it was her plan to start with.

She couldn't go to jail. She wouldn't waste this shot by being stupid.

Shauna Weber thought she was so smart with her fancy education and all her husbands. She'd show her who was the real boss and the smartest woman. *But most important, I'll show her who Patrick really loves.*

The house was on the right, and empty. It had been her idea to pick a time when Shauna was giving another plea to the press. The TV had been talking about it all morning. But they'd held the talk at the Aubrey police station. No one was here in Frisco. No gawkers. No press. And it was hot enough that no one was outside.

At least Patrick could see through the money-hungry bitch he'd married. She'd been so lucky to have met a man like him. And even more lucky that he'd fallen in love with her. If only that stupid wife of his would give him a divorce when he asked.

Her ex's instructions were to put the ransom note in the mailbox when no one was around. It didn't make sense to think no one was watching the house. But she wasn't stupid. She had an idea of her own.

Tory rolled the stroller the opposite way from the Weber house and then down to the driveway to cross the street. She boldly went up to a door and slipped the message behind the screen. Acting like no one was home, she casually walked away without anyone being the wiser.

If Lauren hadn't been alone, she'd be in no hurry to return to the car. But the kid was only four and could get into a lot of trouble by herself. Even locked inside a small bedroom with nothing but a plastic cup and some blocks. Or Tory would have to clean up the accidents. She hated that.

Why did her ex have to get greedy?

It had all been so simple before and would have been over tonight. This was her one time to make it big. So she had no choice. Follow his stupid new plan and somehow keep the ending the same. She'd have her happily ever after with Patrick.

But even then, she might never feel safe if her ex was left alive.

Chapter Eleven

"Please don't hurt our baby. Lauren's just an inno-cent child in all this."

The TV station cut back to the reporter, talking live in front of an empty police station. "That was Shauna Adams Weber, pleading with the kidnap-pers to return her step-granddaughter alive. Kid-napped four days ago from the grocery parking lot, here in Aubrey, Texas. If you've seen this little girl, please call the number on your—"

John clicked the mute button so they wouldn't hear any more of the blather regarding the kidnap-ping. Silent tears rolled down Alicia's cheeks. She sat close enough to the screen to touch the pic-ture of Lauren, almost caressing the beautiful little girl who looked just like her. Long curly dark hair. Freckles across her nose. Same frame. No doubt who that kid's mother was.

"How dare that woman call my child her baby?" Alicia whispered hoarsely.

"So that's the target? The dude standing behind

her doesn't look like much. Why don't I just ask him real polite like?" Dev asked under his breath, and plugged another auxiliary cable into something electronic.

"Negative. Too many unknowns."

"Gotcha. Hey. Isn't that you?" His friend began laughing. "You never said your brother was a twin."

"Turn it up, John."

He did. Knowing they all had to hear the details, but not liking a minute of it.

"With no evidence of a kidnapping and the fleeing of Alicia Ann Adams, police were forced to release Brian W. Sloane earlier this morning. When asked about the kidnapping, Sloane's attorney shrugged and said his client refused to comment."

He hit the mute button. "Give me your cell."

"You could ask," Dev said while reaching into his pants cargo pocket.

"You can leave."

Dev tossed it to his hands. "So demanding," he said to Alicia.

John left the cabin. "Hi, Mabel."

"It's about time we were hearing from you, Johnny. Is this number— Oh, what do they call it on those shows? Secure. Can we talk?"

"Yes, ma'am." He smiled, all the while dreading the conversation with his brother. They hadn't managed more than arguing since he'd returned. "This number's good to reach me. How's Dad doing?"

"He's just fine, Johnny. How's our girl, she safe?"

"Missing Lauren and threatening to beat me to a pulp at every turn."

"Oh, I just bet she is. There's someone here who wants to talk with you." The noise on the phone sounded like it was being passed around. There was a long delay.

"Where are you?" his brother asked.

"You don't need to know."

He'd been expecting his brother, but for some reason hearing himself on the phone had always thrown him for a loop. People thought that being a twin was like seeing yourself in the mirror. It wasn't. In person, the sides of your face are on the wrong side. Hearing himself on the phone was unnerving.

"I see you got out of taking care of dad."

"I'll try to make up for it."

It was hard to explain. Creepy to some. Cool to others. For him, he'd instantly missed the connection with his brother. Maybe he'd been missing it a long time. Though the moment was awkward, it was good. A calm start that neither of them could control. Neither could order the other around.

"They treat you okay in jail?"

"A couple of bruised ribs. Nothing I couldn't handle. Nothing I haven't handled before. One thing they didn't do was talk around me about the investigation. I'm assuming you're the one who figured out they were waiting at Alicia's house to arrest her."

"Yes. Quick thinking to call her instead of your lawyer." *Handled before?* Had the chief or other officers beat his brother?

"I didn't have much time. The deputy had his boot in my back by then. What do you need from me?" Brian asked.

Son of a— What had his brother endured while he'd been gone and why hadn't anyone said anything? *Because I never asked.* "A haircut."

"Already done. Mabel fainted when she walked through the door and I'd used the horse trimmer. Hasn't been this short since we were kids."

In the background there was a distant, "I did not faint, you flirt."

"Stay visible around town, Brian. Let people see you."

"I get it. If they see me, they'll think Alicia really left. Leaving your presence here as a surprise. How do you plan on getting Lauren back?"

"To be honest, I'm not completely sure. But I will." Any luck and Dev would find some property or a money trail. Something. Soon.

"You can't do this alone," Brian said in a low growl.

John recognized the mix of pain, frustration and clenched jaw in the delivery. He spoke that way when he wanted to argue with commands given to him on a mission.

"I've got an expert here. I promise, Alicia's secure and we *will* find Lauren."

"Don't mess this up." Same growl. "A piece of pie from the café might be exactly what we need for dessert after all that chicken, Mabel," he said louder and in a fake worry-free tone. "John." He lowered his voice again. "Weber's as guilty as sin."

"How do you know?"

"I saw him with a chick in Fort Worth one weekend. It wasn't his sister, if you know what I mean. Find her and I bet you'll find Lauren."

"I've got somebody digging into their financials. Did you tell the cops you'd seen him?"

"I didn't bother. They wouldn't believe me, man. Take care of my girls."

"I'll send a message if we find anything."

Brian disconnected. John stuck the phone in his pocket and cracked his neck from side to side. *My girls. Handled before.* Things had changed a lot.

"Did they say anything about Lauren to Brian?" Alicia asked.

He spun around. He'd been so deep in his thoughts he hadn't heard her come outside. That had to stop. "He gave me a lead about Weber."

"Isn't there anything I could be doing? Making phone calls, pretend to check on references or something?"

"Have you thought about how you're going to prove you had nothing to do with this mess?"

"Why? I'm innocent. Why would I have to prove anything? You know I didn't arrange this. You believe me, right?" She plopped onto the porch swing, looking totally defeated.

"What I know doesn't amount to much in court, Alicia." He joined her. "Will you let Dev look into your accounts?"

"What do you expect to find?"

"If Shauna is framing you and Brian for the kidnapping, she might have arranged for more damning evidence."

"I, um… I hadn't thought of that." She began to stand but he caught her arm.

"There's something else."

She waited. Mentally preparing herself for bad news. The expression on her face went from terrible to worse. Tight. Strained. He wanted to be cool with it and not show any emotion one way or the other. At least he thought he did. Jumping out a chopper with a full pack into the Indian Ocean was easier than this conversation.

"I think my brother's in love with you."

"ARE YOU OUT of your ever-loving mind? Brian and I are just friends. We see each other almost every day when leaving instructions or getting leftovers from the fridge. End of discussion." She shook free from his hand.

If she hadn't been so furious, she'd laugh so hard she might fall down. But she was furious. After all these years, John's interpretation was still the same.

"He just told me to take care of his girls."

"When are you going to grow up, Johnny Sloane? It's just an expression."

She jumped to her feet. If she wasn't so exhausted and anxious, she might just give him a dose of reality. Shoot, she was tired enough to go ahead and give him a full heaping helping. "You know this is the same reason neither one of us went to the senior prom. And the same argument we had when we broke up."

"That's not how I remember it."

"You and Brian were arguing. As usual, neither of you said what you really wanted to say. You both interpreted the other and as much as I wanted to stay out of all those stupid arguments, you sucked me in and I didn't ever wear that prom dress."

"You don't know what was going on then. What he thought about me."

"I really thought you'd changed, Johnny. Don't you get it? We were friends. You and Brian both talked to me back then. Both of you. I know both sides of the story. So I think I got the full picture."

"Why aren't you mad at him?" He tensed his body.

"Only one of you left without a word."

"We'd broken up. I didn't think you said you never wanted to talk to me again."

She crossed her arms and tried to stay. Tried to listen. But she needed to get away from him and all the emotion that his return made bubble to the surface. Good or bad emotion, it was just too much.

The words faded the faster she ran, even if she couldn't get far. The cabins sat on the edge of the lake, and she was soon out of path. When she slowed down, she heard the brush crunching. John was directly behind her.

"Don't go off on your own, Alicia. It's not secure."

"It's at least 110 on a weekday. There aren't that many people out here tanning. Actually no one's here to notice me. Is that all you can think about?"

He coolly walked closer. She, as casually as the tension strumming through her would allow, took steps away.

"You have to be careful. Your face is being flashed on every television network and someone's bound to recognize you." He kept his voice low, sounding sexy and dangerous.

"Yours, too."

"It's Brian's, but point taken." He stopped advancing and stretched his arms above his head, yawning. "I don't know if you heard me back there, but I don't know what you mean. You knew I was leaving for the navy. We said goodbye."

What was she supposed to say? "We broke up the night of the fire. I never really thought you'd leave without making things right or that you'd leave without ever coming home." Should she just answer the question that he'd been incapable of verbalizing? "You never asked me wait."

More crashing through the dry leaves had John expertly shoving her behind his body to protect her.

"Dude, you guys can't take off like that. They found another ransom note."

"What?" She'd heard the concern in Dev's voice and asked, "Why would they up the ransom demand on themselves?"

"They wouldn't." John spoke low, sounding more than a little worried. "If they abducted Lauren, they'd want to be the heroes in all this."

"I don't think *they* did. I couldn't record it and don't know them as well as you, Alicia, but they looked genuinely surprised. They kept looking at each other like 'What the frankincense is going on?'"

They all ran back to the cabin. The ransom note was breaking news and being repeated by every local station. So they were able to watch the video replay over and over again. And with each play she fell further into an abyss of despair and hopelessness.

"You're right. They look surprised." Her eyes burned. She wanted to curl into a ball, give up and cry, but that wouldn't accomplish anything. It wouldn't get Lauren back.

"Watch when she turns to him. He shrugs." Dev pointed to Patrick the third time the station played the video behind whatever the broadcasters were saying.

"Or he's shifting his jacket in the heat." John continued his walk around the cabin.

She couldn't call it pacing, per se. He was thinking and moving. He seemed to always move, always be aware. This afternoon, it was walking around the room, tapping the remote with the palm of his hand or rubbing it on the bottom of his chin.

"Dude, unmute it."

"...stunning development. Witnesses say they saw this woman—" the screen flashed an unflattering driver's license picture of her face "—Alicia Ann Adams, mother of the missing little girl, who was thought to be in San Antonio after reservations were discovered in her name. Witnesses report her pushing a stroller with a child through the neighborhood around two this afternoon. The Amber Alert for Lauren Adams continues—"

The TV went silent again.

"Well, we know that's a lie," Dev said. "You've been here. So who's been there?"

"That's the million-dollar question. Any luck running down Weber's phone records and bank accounts?" John asked.

"I can see why the police didn't suspect them. They both look clean." Dev waved them over to look at his laptop screen.

"But…" John added.

"There's a *but?* You really found something?" A spark of hope? It was amazing how fast her mind could latch on to the smallest glimmer that this ordeal might end well.

"Alicia, your accounts aren't so squeaky."

"Mine? I don't understand. I barely had twenty dollars to buy chicken the other night."

"In checking, yes, but your savings account's a different matter." Dev pointed to an insane amount of money.

She looked at both men. "I don't have any savings. I emptied it."

"Actually, you're a cosigner. This account is Lauren's."

That shiny glimmer of hope that had been just out of reach quickly became a far-off pinprick of light in the sky. Again, the images of all those women found guilty in the press… Were any of them ever innocent like her? She couldn't remember hearing of anyone cleared. If she was watching the evidence on television or found this bank account, she'd probably think the mother was horrible and didn't deserve to be reunited with her child.

"Whatever you're thinking, stop." John's hand

was on her shoulder. A strong plea was in his eyes to not give up.

"Don't worry, sister, I'm good at what I do." Dev typed on his laptop.

"Is that a navy SEAL motto?" she asked, trying to put on a brave front. A look shot between the men. Perhaps it was their motto, or they were just surprised they'd both said it.

More screens and code flicked across the monitor. She had no idea what he was doing, but had to trust that he was very good at what he did. John trusted him. And she trusted John to get her daughter back.

"Meanwhile in Dev's world, I've found a couple of rental properties that the Webers' parents own for you two to check out."

She sort of moved through a haze watching John add the addresses to a map application on Dev's phone. The men whispered indiscernibly and she stared at a television now showing the evening programming. She had no point of reference to draw from to try to understand the mind of someone so horrible. No amount of money in the world would make her put an innocent child through this ordeal.

Chapter Twelve

"I thought we were going to check on those two properties Dev told you about. Ponder is the other direction." Alicia pointed west.

"Plenty of time for that." John turned east on Highway 380 and realized they hadn't spoken since pulling away from the cabin. "Finding those properties seemed a little too easy and something the police would have known about. Besides, it's almost dark."

She huffed, crossing her arms and dropping them to her chest.

Did she know she pushed her breasts higher in the air when she did that? If he told her, she'd get embarrassed and stop. He liked it, along with the little puff of air that escaped.

"Please explain your plan."

"Sure. We've all agreed that the Webers seemed surprised at the second ransom demand. Well, what if they're spooked? What if they want to know what's going on and plan on visiting the kidnappers? What if the fake drop is tonight?"

"Do you really think they'll react that way? I mean, surely the police are watching their house, have their phones monitored, et cetera."

"There's always a way. Especially when someone thinks they're smarter than the police."

"I just don't see how—"

"First off—" he hated to bring his world to Alicia's, but he had experience dealing with people she'd never understand "—you should trust me. I've dealt with more than my share of scum who think their plan is foolproof. There's always a way to bring these people down."

"And the second thing?" she asked.

"Don't try to understand them, Alicia. You won't. The price for trying to think like sleazebags is too high. It does something to a person, and you don't deserve that."

He drove Dev's rental for several minutes, watching her peripherally, unable to stop expecting a reaction to his words. An argument? An agreement? More questions? Nothing. Not a hitch in her breathing.

"Is that what happened to you, Johnny?"

"Huh?"

"Do you understand them? The sleaze and scum?" she asked.

"Yeah, I do. Unfortunately."

"I'm sorry."

She pitied him. After everything she'd been through, she pitied *him*. What did anyone say after that conversation? Him? He had nothing, so he kept his trap shut before he said something to confuse their relationship further. He didn't want her to care. He wasn't her problem. When Lauren was back, when his brother was cleared of the charges and when his dad was back on his feet…

There was no reason to care. Hell, Lieutenant Sloane would be out of here and back in a third-world country for another six months. He couldn't afford to care when he'd be right back with the sleaze and scum and away from Alicia's goodness.

Join the navy and rescue strangers all around the world.

Yeah. It didn't surprise him he had no desire to further his military career. The more time he spent here, the less he appreciated his lifestyle of the past twelve years.

Hard to believe it was less than a week ago that he'd received word his dad had suffered a stroke. The first wave that struck him had been relief hearing his dad was still alive. The second, anticipation. His dad's illness justified a confrontation with his brother. He'd no longer needed an excuse to come home.

That hadn't gone as planned.

"How are we supposed to watch a house that's being watched by the police?"

"They won't be expecting us to be watching. That's one thing on our side. The cops are watching Brian hang out in the café. They aren't looking for me here."

"And the cops believe Lauren is safe with me, not kidnapped at all. Do they think I'm sitting around San Antonio, sipping margaritas, waiting for the ransom money to be delivered?"

"I don't think they took it that far, Alicia." He put the car in Park at a stop sign. "That car, second from the end of the block. That's the surveillance team. I can only see one guy in the car, though."

He turned the corner and parked their car a couple of blocks away.

"So what do we do now?" she asked.

"Take a walk."

"You've got to be kidding, John. They've had my face all over the news. What if someone sees me?"

"I need to see the back of the house." *Get closer. Evaluate Weber's expressions, his gestures, his level of anxiety.* But he couldn't get into all the details.

"It's a six-foot fence."

"There's a utility alley between the houses. A six-foot fence means no one will be watching the back for them to leave. No one should notice us and there will be plenty of room for a walk."

"So do you want me to stay here?"

"You're coming with me. A couple is definitely less noticeable." He shoved the pistol Dev had brought him into the back of his pants and opened his door.

"It's okay, no one will see us."

"Leave the gun in the trunk, please."

"Alicia, I know you aren't afraid of pistols."

"We're just a couple out walking. You don't need a gun. If we're noticed, we're running. Right? You wouldn't shoot at the cops."

It wasn't the cops he'd been thinking about. He nodded, wishing he had a piece of gum. Something to chew and work out the nervous tension in his gut. He didn't like venturing into unknown situations. Exposed. Defenseless. He wanted well-thought-out plans to execute, and hated flying by the seat of his pants. That was exactly when things went wrong and someone got killed.

He put the pistol in the trunk and sent a text to Dev, also at Alicia's insistence. His reply couldn't be repeated in polite company.

Feeling naked without a weapon, he laced his fingers through Alicia's. She took a step, but he spun her to face him, drawing her in close so he could lower his voice.

"I say run and you run. No discussion. We'll meet back here at the car. Here's the key." He watched her stuff it into the back pocket of her jeans. "Run means run."

"No debate," she agreed, without convincing him she would follow any directions from him.

"Get the smile out of your eyes, woman. Think about Lauren. The objective is to find her. If we're caught, it'll be a whole lot harder to achieve that goal."

"You're worried?" She gripped his biceps, silently demanding an answer.

"Five days is a long time for kidnappers. They're either feeling confident and getting cocky or they're starting to lose their nerve. My gut tells me they'll make a move soon. Probably tonight."

"I guess I should have asked before now what it is that you do in the navy."

The laugh escaped before he could hold it back. "Let's just say I have experience and you can trust me."

She cupped his cheek with her palm. "Thank you."

He caught himself leaning into her caress and wanting to capture her lips. "Come on."

No one was in sight. No cars parked on this street. People were in their air-conditioned homes with their vehicles locked in their garages. Patrick Weber shouldn't be any different. All the news reports they'd seen had been with the couple standing in their empty driveway. The steps leading up their walk had made it inconvenient to tape them in front of the door.

John had memorized the local landscape this afternoon. Technology and the internet made espionage too easy. The Webers lived on the north side of the street, four houses from the end. At the entrance to the utility ally, John pulled Alicia into his arms again.

"Drop your head against my chest, hon. I need to see over you."

She did as instructed and he verified they were still alone on the street. He grabbed her hand again and darted into the dying weeds. They ran, staying close to the fence. First yard. Second had a dog that barked once or twice. Third yard was behind them. Target yard. No gate. No lights. No noise.

He motioned for Alicia to stay down and close. His eyes were almost level with the top of the fence. He lifted himself to get a full view of the yard.

Professional landscaping and no pool. That would work in his favor. It was only nine o'clock, and yet no lights were on, with the exception of the television glow from the front room. He lowered himself back to Alicia.

"I need you to go back to the car quickly." He placed the phone in her palm. "Pull around to the other end of the alley in six minutes. If I'm not there, go back to the cabin and tell Dev what happened. On the way, call Brian and tell him to get the hell out of Aubrey. When he's sure no one's following him, pick him up somewhere he can leave his truck."

He saw the frightening questions in her expressive eyes and caught the slight shaking of her head. He took her shoulders and whispered, "Nothing's going wrong. You just need to know what to do if it does. I've got this covered."

He kissed her forehead and pointed for her to go.

"Be careful," she said for his ears only.

"Always."

She left the same way they'd come in, remembering the dog and switching to the other side of the alley. He marked his watch with a five-minute countdown. In the corner of the yard, he hopped the fence and got to the back of the house without an alarm sounding.

He slid to the side of the kitchen window and had a perfect view of Shauna stacking bundles of cash into a gym bag. And next to the bag, a set of two keys that would fit a much older truck, reminding him of the one his brother still drove. From Shauna's rich tastes, it didn't seem likely that either of the Webers would be caught dead driving something that old.

He flattened himself to the brick and listened. Shauna left the room. She'd been barefoot, so they weren't leaving immediately. He glanced at his watch. Three minutes. One last glance and he was out of the yard the way he'd come. He hid in the shadows behind a telephone pole until Alicia slowly approached. She didn't come to a full stop as he opened the door and jumped inside.

"My gut was right."

Chapter Thirteen

I'm tracking my daughter's kidnapper. How did this happen?

The surrealism of the situation didn't escape Alicia. She wasn't qualified. Could only do as she was told. And each time she deviated from John's instructions, something bad happened. Her shoes were still wet from the dunking she'd received trying to stop an argument between two men who were on her side.

She couldn't claim to have been doing a wonderful job on her own prior to the kidnapping, but she'd survived. She'd battled all the obstacles of the past four years, and she'd figured it out. Enough that Lauren and she were happy.

I still don't know what to do now.

A couple of minutes driving around in the subdivision and they found the truck on an empty lot at the end of a cul-de-sac. They parked in view of the subdivision entrance to watch for the truck to leave.

John convinced her to drive, since he had other

things to prep. He retrieved his gun, stuffed it into his waistband and texted Dev. He sat next to her, leaning back in the seat, keeping watch and thumbing through screens on the smartphone. She was so anxious to get Lauren back she could hardly think about any of the details he'd been going over.

"Are you playing solitaire? How can you be completely confident this is going to work?" she asked after forty-five minutes.

"I'm never *completely* confident. Solitaire keeps me from thinking about things that can go—"

"Wrong." There was a long list of things that could go "south," as he constantly put it.

John put a hand on her shoulder, deeply massaging the tight muscles. "You're tense. Relax. The steering wheel can't possibly escape that death grip of yours."

Two cars passed and had her leaning forward, jumping to start the car. John's hand stayed her from turning the key. Her heart beat so quickly she checked the mirror to see if the vein in her throat was bulging. She rubbed her shaking hands up and down her thighs, feeling the adrenaline tremble through her body.

Doubt crammed into her mind and blocked her ability to think straight. She had to know if she was as clueless as she felt.

"Did I miss something? Could I have prevented

the kidnapping or bank transfers or any of this from happening?"

"No," John answered quickly, but stiffened.

"How can you be so certain?" Questioning her movements and decisions was a big part of the apprehension building inside her chest. If he knew something... If he had an answer... Maybe that would ease the tension and allow her to function better.

He shifted uncomfortably. His gaze seemed to drift. Then he looked sad, like a memory he didn't want to face wouldn't leave him alone. She'd seen that faraway look a couple of times now. He was physically fit and looked like Brian, so she'd sort of *seen* him for twelve years. But something big in him had changed. She'd known Johnny. This man was Lieutenant Sloane. She didn't know him at all.

"Whoever kidnapped Lauren, they've thought this through and planned her abduction for a long time. Framing you and Brian took months. I think they planned for you to die in the car. Then the Webers would rescue your daughter and have custodial control over the trust fund without any questions."

As hot as the evening still was, her skin was covered in goose bumps. He'd spoken with chilling reality, logic and confidence.

I think they planned for you to die, his voice echoed in her head.

The sheriff had said something like that, too.

And still, she'd shrugged it off, been optimistic, unable to think the worst, and she definitely didn't want to believe Shauna could really hate her that much.

"Your theory makes perfect sense. I just can't begin to think like you and I'm so grateful you came home. Without you, I'd be in jail and lost to Lauren forever."

"Don't think about that possibility. Besides, why should a nurse who spends her time caring for others think like me? I'm glad you can't wrap your mind around this situation. Really glad. I like who you grew up to be."

"Are they going to hurt her? Be straight with me, Johnny."

"I don't know. If you concentrate on the unknowns, it sort of makes you crazy. Just remember that we *will* get her away from them."

No tears. Not even a threat of them. She was all cried out. Too worried about making another mistake. John twisted to face her, taking her chin in his fingers, nudging her to stare from the street toward him.

"Wherever they lead us—if they go at all—you know there's no guarantee Lauren will be there." The crease between his brows grew prominent with his concern. "If she is, it might get messy. Maybe I should drop you off and—"

"No. I'll do anything necessary to keep my

daughter safe. Don't worry about me. I've been on my own for a while now." And she had. Her father, Dwayne's accident and then her father-in-law. "Talk about something else while we wait."

"Dev said the money in Lauren's savings was a series of small cash deposits over the last four months. Different branches. Nothing electronic."

"Alicia, you okay?" he asked after a minute of silence.

"I'm fine."

"I wanted to ask before, but where's your dad and brother through all this? I expected them to show up sooner."

"Alzheimer's. Dad had a slow progression in the beginning. I took care of him as long as I could. But he doesn't recognize me anymore. He mistook me for Mom for a while. But he hasn't had many lucid moments in a very long time. He was in a nice place in Denton, but when Shauna got me fired, I had to move him to a state facility about four hours from here."

"I'm sorry, I didn't know." His large hand covered hers, squeezing. "My dad never mentioned it. I shouldn't have brought it up."

"It's okay. You didn't know. J.W. was pretty upset. He lost his two best friends in a short amount of time. My brother's never been close and is stationed in Germany. He volunteered to go shortly after Dad needed round-the-clock care, and I haven't called him about Lauren. It doesn't make sense. What could he do?"

"Alicia, I can't begin to understand what you've been through. What about Roy? Dad said he died from a broken heart. I asked what that meant, but he never said."

"He shot himself three months after Dwayne's accident."

"Son of a— That can't be true. They're certain? Who found him?"

"Shauna." She hated saying the woman's name. It was bad enough thinking about her. "This isn't exactly the subject to help relax me." She forced a short nervous laugh and relaxed her fingers again.

"You're right. That was stupid of me."

"What are we going to do when we follow them to where they have Lauren?"

"There's no *we*. I'll go inside and do what's necessary. You'll stay in the car and call Dev if something goes wrong."

"I can help. Believe me."

"I'm sure you can, but we're going to have to grab Lauren and hightail it into hiding."

"I don't understand. Why can't we just go home? Or at least to the county sheriff. He'll believe us. We have to tell someone what we know and let the police arrest them."

"We haven't proved that you didn't orchestrate this from the start. It's their word against yours."

"But Lauren can tell everyone the truth."

"No, that won't work. At this point, you won't win."

She was stunned into silence. Where could she take Lauren that was safe? How would they survive without any money? It didn't matter. She meant what she'd said. She was willing to do anything to get Lauren back. That included becoming a fugitive and hiding until she could prove her innocence.

"You need to prepare yourself for another scenario."

His tragic tone shouted and screamed *what if.*

"No, don't say it. Don't think it. I won't accept that they could hurt her."

"Alicia. We have to be reasonable."

"Wait. Isn't that the truck?"

She started the car, putting it in Drive after the truck passed and they knew which direction he was heading. The older truck could have been mistaken for the one Brian drove. Very distinguishable among the newer models on the road. It made it easy to keep two or three cars between them and not lose sight of its direction.

"Looks like Patrick's alone. Why would he pay them without Shauna?" Alicia asked.

"Probably the same reason I should be alone right now. It's dangerous."

They followed on the main road, being led farther away from the larger cities and even small towns. Onto rural roads, where it was harder to keep the truck in sight without giving their presence away. Sometimes they depended solely on the vehicle lights ahead of them in the distance. Then brakes.

"Alicia, can you see the road in the dark?"

"I think so." The sandy gravel reflected enough moonlight that she could see and not drive into the ditch.

"He's slowing down," John confirmed. "Stop here. It must be the driveway of a house." He tapped the phone and put it to his ear. "Dev, I need info on a property. Just texted coordinates….Extraction. Solo….Negative….No, I can't wait. No second pair of eyes. She'll be secure in the car."

She was amazed at how matter-of-fact every aspect of Lauren's rescue was to John. Was this what he did as a SEAL? *Where will you be safe, Johnny?*

"Hide the car," he mumbled as he pointed. "See that spot behind us where the side of the road is flatter? We need to get behind those trees."

"But there's a fence. Won't the car still be in the road?"

"Not for long. And you're staying in it. You promised to follow orders." John reached into his pocket, then jumped from the car.

By the time she'd reversed onto level ground, he'd cut the barbed wire and she could park it in the field hidden from other drivers. He pulled the wire mostly back together and motioned for her to join him. The truck hadn't moved from next to the mailbox.

"Stay close to the car and keep this." He handed her the phone. "There's a map of the area and you'll be able to let Dev know where to pick you up. You can trust him."

"I'm going with you."

He just shook his head and smiled. "Not this time, sweetheart. I'm in. I get Lauren. I'm out."

"What are you—"

John cut off her words with a quick kiss. Not supersexy, but the surprise was effective and shut her up.

"I can't wait to explain. I want in before Patrick. I'll be back soon with your daughter."

John ran. His dark T-shirt and jeans were stark against the light brown of drying hay. The large round hay bales set randomly throughout the field gave him the cover he needed to avoid being seen. Hopefully.

She had to do something. She couldn't just sit and wait. But what, she had no idea. No frame of reference. No experience. Only one thing—Lauren was her daughter.

Thank God this man had come back home. If it weren't for him, she'd have no way to prove Shauna's involvement. And no one to save Lauren.

Too antsy to stay in one place, she wanted to

view the map sent earlier. She darted across the road out of view, ducking behind the bushes until no lights from the house could be seen.

Oh, no. There were more headlights slowly turning from the main road. Like a car wanting to remain unseen or a person who might be lost. She ran hard, making her lungs hurt. Across the rows of dirt and grass until she could hide in the trees.

The car turned the curve and went dark. It took several seconds to pass the bend in the road and roll to a stop close to the drive. Alicia could make out only the silhouette of a head. It didn't take someone with John's experience to understand whoever was inside that second car didn't want to be seen.

The person in the car was waiting. The sound of the engine filled the silence. Had Patrick been followed? Had she and John been followed? Or was the stranger Shauna and this part of their plan all along?

The car loomed like a demon waiting to pounce. *What are you up to?* It didn't matter.

John was nowhere in sight. She had no way to contact him and he wouldn't know about this additional danger. Patrick finally drove his truck toward the house. She had to help John, so she ducked farther into the brush and covered the brightness of the phone. The map appeared on the screen.

The objective was to stop these people from hurting Lauren. No matter what happens.

Chapter Fourteen

John crossed the hay field without any problem. He approached straight down the fencerow next to the drive, using the trees as cover.

There were actually two old houses, both probably built before indoor plumbing. The southern one closest to him, just a box with steps, had no lights and no activity. Storm cellar to its east. Barn to the north, then a shed, tractor and some baled hay.

Between him and the main house was a circular drive with a large oak in dead center. All laid out just like the gridded map in his head.

The larger house had started small with rooms haphazardly stuck to it. One of those additions was definitely the bathroom. He could see pipes and a hole in the ground from plumbing work. Two he could assume were bedrooms. They each had a small window air-conditioning unit identical to the one in the front room.

Weber had taken his sweet time pulling up the driveway. He parked near the smaller house and was still in the dang truck. No one reacted to his arrival. No doubt due to the window unit and blaring television.

A blind rescue. He hated being without intel on how many assailants were inside or where the hostage was located. What he wouldn't give for some heat imaging to locate hostiles.

When Weber finally got out of the old truck, he was covered from head to toe, including gloves. Not good. It had to be almost a hundred degrees still. Obviously, he didn't want to leave evidence behind. The situation had all the markers of going south fast.

Pictures. Video. Why hadn't he brought Dev's cell to record the exchange? He'd thought only of rescuing Lauren, and that Alicia needed the phone for her safety. Nothing else. It was too far to run back and retrieve the thing. He'd taken images of Weber in the truck, but a recorded conversation would be damning and convict the Webers, clearing Alicia. It couldn't be explained away as easily as a ride in an old truck.

After the rescue, mother and daughter would be together. At least that met his priority objective.

Weber appeared nervous and hesitant walking up the steps to the wide well-lit porch. He shifted the gym bag from shoulder to shoulder. If he and Shauna had nothing to do with the kidnapping, delivering the ransom without police involvement wasn't a good idea. They had to be guilty.

Then where's the money? Dev was the best, and he was having problems finding it.

The outside light flicked on. Weber was greeted by a surprised young woman. A man yelled. As soon as he walked inside, an argument began. Indistinguishable words, but John could guess what it concerned.

John darted behind the darkened house, pausing at the raised earth of the cellar. No outside guard. No one standing watch. No cattle or horses in the field. No dogs and not even a sign of a cat. He zigzagged the open twenty yards to the corner of the bathroom.

Words like *in charge* and *highfalutin* popped through the thin walls, along with a host of four-letter words. Unless Patrick Weber's voice had shifted from a tenor to a deep bass, the man he'd joined wasn't a happy camper. Weber showing up—especially without the extra cash—wasn't to their liking. But neither was the surprise demand for more. The way the men discussed the details was additional proof that Lauren's step-grandparents were in charge of the entire kidnapping. But there still wasn't evidence that would clear Alicia or Brian.

John kept his back to the paint-peeling wood, glancing into the windows of each room. At the rear of the house, one of the window units had plywood over the glass. *Bingo.* Lauren had to be in that room. The wood was new and the nailing sloppy, but he couldn't pry it loose with just his hands or the multitool that lived in his back pocket. There wasn't anything lying around to help. He couldn't risk losing time searching the barn.

Just past the window was another porch. Kitchen. Back door. He tried the knob. Unlocked. He cracked it open. No squeak.

Weapon ready, John crept inside, leaving the door open behind him, and silently got his back to the cabinets near the main room. Only one way into the rest of the house. In fact, there weren't any hallways. All the rooms opened onto the front room, where everyone was located.

"You ain't gettin' the kid till I get the rest of the dough," the second man screamed.

The yelling grew louder. More erratic. Covering several subjects. About staying in an old rattrap of a house. About Tory, the woman who had answered the door. About how tired he was of babysitting a kid. The woman screamed back, seeming to hold her own until the big guy backhanded her. And Weber remained silent, looking edgy.

The anxiety landing in the pit of John's gut wasn't good. This second man seemed to be strung out— no telling what drug he was high on or what he was capable of doing. Tory kept trying to appease him, calm him.

It didn't work. And after a second brutal slap, she pressed against the wall and out of his reach. Getting Lauren out of the house fast was imperative.

"Take the money," Weber encouraged. "There's twenty-five grand here."

"We decided we need more, and you gotta pay to keep us shut up."

"Then leave it." Weber shrugged.

John surveyed the living room via a wall mirror he could see from where he stood. The girl was blond, petite and had a deeply black eye. There were bruises up and down her arms.

"Come on, babe. This is what we've waited for." The girl tugged on the man's arm. "Twenty-five thousand gets us on a beach in the Bahamas."

"Stop hanging on me, you whore." He propelled her away and she collided with the TV stand. The old set crashed to the floor and Weber didn't cringe or react. "I told you, you ain't getting the kid for less than half a mil."

"You're certain about that?" Weber dropped the bag from his shoulder.

John heard the zipper. Did Weber really think he could convince this guy to take the money by showing it to him? Aw, hell. There must be a gun in the top of the bag.

Should he wait for Weber to draw and hope the big guy could defend himself? Then he'd proceed to where he thought Lauren could possibly be located.

Or should he stop Weber before he killed the only two people who could prove Alicia's innocence?

"Hold it." John spun around the corner and aimed his 9 mm at Weber.

"Who the hell are you?" The big man took a step closer to him.

"Far enough." John shifted his aim between the two men. The second was easily five inches taller than John and outweighed him by a good eighty pounds. The man was a damn giant.

"What are you doing here, Sloane?" Weber asked.

"You know this bastard?" the other man said to Weber, but advanced toward John.

"Stay back and, Weber, show me your hands." He gestured with the gun for them to move to the outside wall. "Slowly stand up and back away from the bag."

"I'm going to tear you both to shreds."

"Back to your corner, Gargantuan." He kept both men in his view, but lost sight of Tory. Served him right if something hit him over the head for being so careless, but it wouldn't help Lauren.

"You should leave. I'm here to get the kid back and you're mucking everything up." Weber stood, but suspiciously slipped his hand into his pocket.

"I know why you're here, and it won't work."

"I disagree." Weber dived for the bag, rolled and fired.

John couldn't discharge his weapon for the same

reason he'd tried to prevent Weber from shooting. He couldn't risk injuring Lauren or the kidnappers. But that wouldn't stop the others from taking the risk.

When Weber dived toward the front door, Gargantuan dived straight into John. The woman who cowered in the corner scurried in the opposite direction. John lost sight of Weber when a thick shoulder hit his kidney, stunning him with the force. He kept his grip on his gun, hitting the giant of a man in the side of the head.

Gargantuan didn't flinch, just locked his arms around John's midsection and started squeezing. He wasn't just huge, he absorbed all the hard-hitting blows John could deliver. The deadlock around his ribs had him struggling for air. He couldn't get any traction with his feet dangling. Then the giant shoved him into the wall.

The gun flew while old picture frames banged to the floor. John watched his defense land close to the front door. Hand to hand it would have to be.

John used his legs to do his own shoving. They both shot across the room. Gargantuan lost his balance but not his grip as they crashed between the chair and couch. John could only see the nicotine-yellowed ceiling, but the voice of a child was very distinct behind one of the doors.

"Help."

ALICIA RAN TO the farm, imitating John's movements, and following as much of the path as she'd watched earlier. The car she came to warn John about was still parked—waiting for something. Just like when they'd run from the house that morning, she got close to the fence and tried to blend in with the trees. Once she reached the open yard, she skirted around the edge of the houses before getting close to the back porch.

The door was open. She heard thrashing inside and then distinct sounds of a car door out front. Could John already have Lauren?

JOHN THRUST HIS elbow under Gargantuan's ribs. Again. Then again.

Blessed relief around his chest was followed with direct hits simultaneously to his ears. He saw two women—or maybe it was one and he was seeing double—twist a dead bolt on one of the doors.

They were moving Lauren. He had to get free.

A quick shake of his head, attempting to clear it, just made the double vision worse. His ears burned as much as his anger at being taken by surprise by Weber's bully. And Weber.

He flipped around and landed a couple of punches to a massive chest. He saw the woman running, dragging Lauren behind her. Escaping.

Time to end this.

AFRAID SOMEONE WAS leaving with Lauren, Alicia ran around the house to stop them. The porch light was enough to see Patrick running to the driveway, waving an arm above his head. He carried a bag, but didn't have Lauren. She stayed in the dark at the edge of the porch. Should she go in the house? Where was John?

More crashing. Shadows of bodies hit the curtains. Two men were fighting. It must be John. She searched the darkness, trying to get her eyes to adjust to find Patrick, but he'd disappeared. A car—most likely the one from the road—was headed toward the house.

A tiny, frightened whimper. Alicia's attention snapped to the porch.

"Patrick, wait," a woman shouted, shoving the screen door against the wall as she ran through.

"Lauren." Though a little dirty, her daughter seemed uninjured.

"Mommy! Mommy!" Lauren struggled to free her wrist from a familiar young woman. The struggling forced the woman to pause and get control. When Lauren couldn't get free, her daughter threw herself to the porch, taking her captor to her knees and turning her face toward Alicia.

"Tory?"

GARGANTUAN WOULDN'T STAY DOWN. John threw his head backward, connecting with the man's nose.

He heard the familiar crunch of cartilage breaking and took advantage of his opponent's momentary stunned state to scramble to his feet.

Twelve years in the navy had taught him a couple of things about hand-to-hand combat. It was time to let some of it kick into high gear. There was no guilt at a few dirty tricks to get this kidnapper on the floor.

Another punch caught him in the chin, but he returned with three quick jabs of his own. He hit a bloody nose twice, obtaining a groan of pain from his opponent. He spun, kicked, connected. Boot sliced flesh.

Gargantuan finally looked dazed. Another kick to the head. He fell through the kitchen doorway and didn't get up.

Where the hell is my gun?

ALICIA WATCHED AS Tory waved the handgun like an inexperienced teenager afraid of what she held. She yanked Lauren onto her side, the gun so close she could accidentally hit her little girl.

Lauren squirmed on Tory's hip.

"Be still!" the frightened young woman shouted. "Stay away. Just stay back."

"It's okay, princess." Alicia tried to sound calm while coaxing her baby to keep out of the line of fire. "Stay there and be still, sweetheart. Do what Tory says."

"I don't want to stay with her no more, Mommy."

"Shut up," Tory hysterically screamed, pounding the gun against her skull. "I can't think what I need to do."

"Princess, please be still and let me see if Miss Tory will let you come home."

"That ain't never goin' to happen. Not until—Patrick?" Tory searched the dark, the gun pointed casually toward Lauren again. "God, Patrick, don't leave me."

Nervous, anxious, uncertain… Alicia shoved a stopper into those emotions before they clouded her judgment. But whatever she felt, Tory was horrifically worse. She'd clearly been beaten and was terrified. She searched the yard, pointing the gun practically everywhere, including at Lauren.

Alicia couldn't wrap her mind around who held the hand of her daughter. Shauna had to be responsible for the kidnapping. Tory worked for minimum wage at Mary's day care. She didn't have enough money or influence to create a money trail that would frame her.

It was Shauna. It had to be.

"We're going to get in that car and drive away from here." Tory wrapped Lauren tightly across the front of her body, using her daughter as a human shield. "Do you hear me, Alicia? Nobody comes near me or I'll shoot. I don't want to, but I will."

Lauren cried, chanting, "Mommy, Mommy, Mommy."

It broke her heart not to sprint to Tory and lock her daughter into a tight embrace of love.

"You don't have to do this, Tory. We can work things out. No one will ever know."

Flashing police lights spun into the night near where they'd left the rental. Lights from the car that had been lurking for so long popped to life at the end of the driveway, heading toward the house.

"It's too late. I'm not going to jail. I'm sorry, but Lauren's my only chance."

"Don't be crazy, Tory. Patrick and Shauna have to be behind this. All you have to do is tell the police what happened. You can make a deal."

Tory took the steps to the yard fast and ran to the parked car. "I'm not going to jail. Stay there. I swear I'll shoot." Her voice was full of panic as she jerked the gun around, her finger on the trigger, Lauren still in her arms. "We're going."

"Mommy, please," Lauren sobbed. Frightened tears streamed down her little cheeks as her hands stretched past her captor toward Alicia.

Alicia watched in horror as Tory tripped and fell behind the car. She heard a petrified scream from her little girl. Gun or no gun, she ran to rescue her daughter.

On the far side of the car, two bodies struggled, outlines until the beams from the car drew closer. Tory sat on John's chest, a crazed look on her face, her hands swiping at him like bobcat claws.

"Go. Find your daughter. I've got this," John said as he locked his long fingers around one of the wrists still slapping at him.

Lauren was nowhere in sight. She couldn't help him; she had to find her daughter.

"Lauren! Where are you, princess?" she called with no success. "Are you hurt? Lauren, baby, where are you?"

Movement at the edge of the darkness, near the trees. Lauren. Headlights momentarily blinded her before the car cut her off from her baby.

"Mommy, help me."

"Get her, dammit," Shauna shrieked from the driver's seat.

Alicia ran, following her daughter's wails. Near the car that had just stopped, she saw Patrick grab Lauren from her hiding place under his parked truck and lift her into his arms, slapping a hand over her mouth to keep her quiet. She started to run toward them and the car door opened, broadsiding Alicia to the ground, knocking her breath from her lungs.

"No! I don't want to go with you. I want my mommy."

A shot echoed between the house and trees.

Oh, my God. The last she'd seen, Tory had the gun and had been struggling with John. But she had to get Lauren before Patrick left with her.

"Baby." Alicia rolled away from the car door to her knees. Just as her feet were under her, she was pulled back to the ground. *John.* Relief blasted through her as sharply as that shot had pierced the night.

"Let me go."

On the ground with her, he clapped a hand across her mouth to keep her quiet, but kept them moving to the edge of the house. "Don't fight me. We can't get her. Believe me."

The police sirens blasted into the yard. The cars stopped, blocking the drive at the top of the circle. John half dragged, half rolled Alicia into the complete blackness cast by the house's shadow. He covered her with his body and waited. What was he doing? She had to get Lauren.

"Thank God you're here. It was them." Shauna yelled at both officers who approached her. "They're here. She was just here with her junkie boyfriend. Find and arrest them before they get away!"

There was no way to escape, lying under him. He remained motionless and didn't bother to relieve some of the heaviness of his muscled body, which cut off her oxygen.

She could still see the charade being played out in front of her eyes. An intense drama with no comic relief or happy ending in sight.

Chapter Fifteen

"Is she dead?" Shauna asked the first officer who pulled up, now kneeling by Tory.

From next to the house, John had a decent view of the action playing out in the driveway. Just like the situation he'd been in a couple of years back when a buddy got wounded with hostile fire on both sides. He clamped his hand tightly over Alicia's mouth and froze.

No movement. No sound. It was crucial not to draw attention to themselves right now. If they did, they might as well surrender. He didn't surrender.

"Hang tight or they'll see us," he whispered directly into her ear.

"See when backup's going to get here," the older officer commanded his much younger counterpart. "Then check the house without destroying all the evidence."

Patrick Weber stared at the woman lying there, motionless. He didn't utter a sound or show any remorse.

"Shouldn't we look for those other two who got away?" The younger officer drew his weapon and walked directly to where John was trying to control a squirming Alicia.

"Do what I said," the older officer yelled, reversing the younger guy in his tracks. "We've rescued the girl and can't leave the scene."

Shauna ran to Weber and jerked Alicia's daughter from her husband's arms. "Oh, Lauren, thank God we found you."

Weber walked a little less hesitantly to the rear of his truck and dropped the tailgate. John could no longer see his face, but he saw a puff of smoke. The distinct smell of cigarettes drifted to their hiding place.

Lauren looked surprisingly like a miniature Alicia. Her face was grimy and tear streaked, clothes filthy, curly hair a tangled mess. The kid definitely had the will to fight like her mother. She squirmed, tugged on hair and slapped. When Shauna swatted her behind, Lauren silently cried, drawing in huge gulps of air around her two middle fingers she'd stuck in her mouth.

He hoped Alicia couldn't see what was happening. If he could, he'd cover her ears to keep her from hearing, too. What if Lauren cried for her again?

"Let me up," Alicia mumbled, twisting violently under him and moving until she could whisper clearly. "It's over. Lauren's safe. We caught them with those kidnappers. They can be arrested. All we have to do is give ourselves up."

"Nothing's over," John whispered. "Surrendering is not an option."

"I don't understand. You can't let them— I've got to get to Lauren." She spoke strongly into his ear.

"We still don't have any proof you're innocent."

"Nonsense. You can't keep me here, John Sloane. She needs me."

"Your daughter needs you for longer than it takes to put you in handcuffs." He replaced his hand over her mouth. "I'm not letting you go. Period. The younger one is so skittish, he may shoot us on sight."

Her body went limp in defeat, not moving, with the exception of the silent crying. Good. He needed to find a safe way back to the car. They were too close to Tory's body to make a run for the fence line. They'd be heard or seen before they could get out of sight. If either officer walked the perimeter of the circular driveway, they'd be discovered before they got to their knees.

The extraction route would be the back of the main house, then the barn and out through the far pasture. It would take longer, but it was the only way.

Shauna pivoted from the dead woman, meeting the younger officer at his car. "I agree with you.

Alicia and Brian need to be found and caught. Are you really not going after them? They can't be far. They were just here when you pulled up. If you don't hurry, they'll get away."

Her daughter fought Shauna just as hard as Alicia fought for her own freedom while pinned beneath him. As difficult as it must be for her to draw a breath with his two hundred pounds on her back, she gathered strength and tried to throw him off several times. He jerked a little when she tried nipping at his fingers. He ignored it and kept her snug to the ground, not trusting her to break free and take off after Lauren.

"Orders, ma'am." The young officer holstered his weapon and leaned into the car, grabbing the radio.

"I want my mommy!"

Alicia's body jerked under him. She bucked violently trying to get free.

"But they're getting away," Shauna whined, and returned her attention to the older officer still at the side of Tory's body. "You *have* to go after them. This little girl isn't safe. None of us are safe."

"Stand back, Mrs. Weber. I've told you we have to wait here." The older officer spoke loudly over Lauren's cries.

"You're just going to let them escape?" Shauna harped.

"Don't worry about that. We'll set up road blocks and get them before they leave the county," the officer in charge said. "So you got a good look at them?"

"It was them, Brian and Alicia. Oh, my God, he just shot that woman. I can't believe it. She…she… I think she worked at Lauren's day care, and must have helped them, but she didn't deserve to die. Brian just turned the gun and shot her point blank when she tried to get away."

"We'll find them, Mrs. Weber." The older officer spoke loudly over the cries of the four-year-old. "Weren't you instructed when you phoned earlier to wait for our arrival before approaching the kidnappers?"

Shauna should have gone to Hollywood after graduation. She never skipped a beat. "If you hadn't taken so long we wouldn't be in danger now."

Lauren pulled Shauna's hair.

"Ow! You stup— Don't be a bratty child." She said the words, but looked at the officer as she held Lauren as far from her body as possible.

The officer in charge stood and placed a hand on Lauren's back, patting her, then held out his arms. Lauren went to him without any coaxing. He walked in circles, trying to calm her sobbing.

"When they turn their backs to us, we're going," John whispered. With all the distractions in front of the house, they could crawl safely to the back side of the barn.

"No." He felt her mouth form the word beneath

his palm and felt the defeat rip through Alicia's torso. She struggled to push him from her.

John couldn't lessen his grip around her waist. There was no way he'd let her go. Gargantuan hadn't left by the front door and was probably in the woods by now. Weber hadn't told the cops he'd seen the big guy in the house, so the police wouldn't be looking for him. But the giant would definitely be looking for them.

With the death of the young woman who had taken Lauren, it was evident the Webers had no intention of leaving anyone alive who stood between them and the money. Until the money was legally in their control, Lauren was safe.

No one faced their direction.

John stood, tugging Alicia farther into the darkness, and she lashed out at him the entire way. He had to throw her over his shoulder before running behind a hay bale near the barn. He let her slide down his chest, back to the ground.

She took a step toward the circular drive. John clamped his arm around her thin waist and tugged her face into his shoulder. He'd watched the artificial way Lauren was being held. It broke his heart, but not half as much as Alicia's if he let her see it. There was nothing he could do.

"Now's not the time. It's suicide if we go back there."

It would be easier if she was unconscious. He'd

had to do that once before on a rescue. It had been absolutely necessary and had saved six lives. But John had never forgiven himself for hitting the hysterical hostage to knock him out. No way could he hit Alicia.

Shauna's show of hysterics continued as she ranted to the younger officer, telling him not to listen to his superior. The officer issuing orders still held a crying Lauren. It was enough of a distraction without any help. Then she ran to Weber demanding he do something or chase them himself. When he stood, both officers raced to the tailgate.

They'd be in the clear for a solid couple of minutes, with the argument commencing. So long as they could make it behind the barn and possibly across the field. He caught Alicia's attention and pointed to the next hay bale, then gave a hand signal that they'd run in three, two—

"I can't leave her," she pleaded. "John, please. You have to get Lauren. Do something."

"Don't argue with me."

He ordered his heart to ignore her pleas. He didn't know how much time they had before the police backup arrived. He'd get Lauren. He just couldn't at this particular moment. There were too many unknown variables. Only one gun, one clip, one chance at their vehicle. And if a cop discovered the rental on their way to the scene, they'd be stuck in the backwoods. Even if they managed to make the main road and call for an extraction, the rental would be discovered and they'd know John was in Texas via his best friend's name on the agreement.

Bottom line—he needed that anonymity edge to ensure Alicia was safe whether she liked it or not. He dragged her along with him until they were far enough away for her to concede. She ran next to him—silent, quick, physically okay. He knew she'd have a hard time forgiving his failure.

"We've got to get out of here before additional cops show up." He said it sternly. Whether for her benefit or to ease his conscience about leaving Lauren behind, he didn't know. He would assure her somehow that he'd rescue her daughter soon.

The car was where they'd left it, key in the ignition, phone on the seat. He went to remove the cut fence and she latched on to his arm.

"You're really not going back for her?"

He shook his head, unable to utter the word *no,* which had stuck in his throat. The defeat washed over her like a spray from a water hose, drenching her belief in him faster than that dousing in the lake.

"I thought you were a hotshot navy SEAL. You can help strangers all over the world but not my daughter." She shoved him away, covering her face to hide the silent tears.

The dig caught him unaware and right in his vulnerable spot. Around the world, but never at home. Same opinion Brian had of him.

She ran to the wire and yanked it back while he moved branches out of the way. He started the ignition and crept the car from the field. Once around the corner, he bolted down the dirt road, constantly watching for an approaching vehicle.

Their luck held and they were on the main road in less than three minutes.

"She begged me to help. How could you just leave her? What am I going to do now?" Alicia pressed her palms to her eyes, turned to the window. "How will she ever forgive me?"

John asked himself the same question about Alicia.

It took all his restraint not to turn the car around, rush onto the scene and remove Lauren by force. He wanted to swear he would—right then—or swear that he'd bring Lauren back no matter what. But he'd taken that oath before and been unable to keep it. She'd find out sooner or later that he wasn't the hero she needed.

John drove around the corner and continued another mile before turning on the headlights and calling Brian.

His brother answered Mabel's cell on the first ring. "Did you find Lauren?"

"Mabel's with you?"

"Why?"

"You need an alibi," John stated, thinking the same four-letter words his brother muttered into the phone.

"Did something happen to Lauren or Alicia?"

"No. We prevented whatever they had planned. We were also close to getting caught. There was a confrontation and I underestimated the opposition."

"Explain."

He recounted everything he'd seen, even that he had no idea why Alicia had followed him to the house. A vague idea that she'd never keep her promise to follow orders. Not that it mattered to the way he'd messed things up. But she might not be shutting down if she hadn't seen just how close he'd been to Lauren without rescuing her.

"Shauna identified us. Naming you and Alicia as the kidnappers. I need to find a place that's safe while I clear Alicia's name. You need to delete Mabel's call history. The police can access it eventually, but it'll take a warrant instead of just a glance. It'll slow them down awhile. Give us some time to finish this thing."

"Got it. I'm assuming this is the last call for a while. I activated Dad's cell this afternoon. Use that number to call or text. You know, if Tory worked at the day care, I should be able to check her out. Maybe I can find out who this giant is. You said he stunk like horses? Only twenty or more horse ranches in the area."

"Alicia seemed to know her, but stay clear of it, Brian. I've got someone who can handle searching for info." He glanced at his silent passenger. Still crying. She hadn't uttered a word.

"That huge monster beat the girl up. Regularly. Fresh bruises on her face."

"Does Alicia recognize him?"

"I don't think she got a look at him."

"Did anyone actually see you?" Brian asked.

"If anyone did, it was Weber, but you shouldn't—"

"I was at the diner until it closed. Plenty of witnesses to back that up. No way I could get to the McKinney area to fight Weber's man. Mabel's here to verify what time I got home."

"I was so close, Brian."

"Do you need help? I've got a place where I stay in Fort Worth they don't know about."

"They'll be all over you even with the alibi." He watched Alicia out of the corner of his eye, wishing he knew what to do. "We should be fine. I need to make a call and will get back to you with details or if something else happens."

"Gotta go. Looks like the police chief is pulling up."

Alicia hadn't moved. He reached across her and snapped her seat belt. He needed to call Dev soon. That had been the plan. But he was disappointed in his personal failure. He'd let this woman down, badly.

"What's going to happen now?" she asked and sniffed, wiping her face.

"I'm not sure. We need to see what the locals do and regroup."

"You should have let me go to her."

"The police wouldn't have treated you well, Alicia. There was nothing either of us could do. You understand that, right?

"I don't want to talk about it," she said with another sniff.

"But we have to."

"Did you shoot Tory?"

"Do you think I'd shoot her?"

"I… I'm— I didn't think you'd walk away and leave Lauren there, either." She shook her head, dropping her face in her hands again. "I don't know what to think. You're not the same man I knew twelve years ago."

"I hope I'm not. I was just a kid without a good head on my shoulders, who took advantage of his brother." *Not for the reasons everyone believes, but I still took advantage of his admission.* "Dammit, I didn't *want* to leave your daughter with those people."

He had no more explanations. *Excuses, you mean.* Better word choice, more accurate. Poor planning. Caught with his pants down. Disbelief when the woman sitting on him fell to her side, shot in the head. The strong emotions associated with this op overpowered his ability to think straight.

"For the record, I didn't shoot anyone. My weapon hasn't been fired. Check it." He leaned forward, pulled it from his back waistband and held it out to her. She'd been cleaning handguns since she could pull a trigger and knew what to do without any instruction, but she didn't take it from him. "It's a safe bet that Weber used one of Brian's or even Dwayne's."

"Patrick shot her? But when I heard the shot, he was holding Lauren. You mean she heard, maybe even saw him?" She tugged on his arm. "Turn around. Now. I'm begging you not to leave her with them. Oh, dear God. What are they going to do to her?"

"She's safe." *For now, at least.*

They couldn't go back. She acknowledged that in a matter of seconds with a deep, hurtful roar of hopelessness. It didn't matter that he was the person who'd made the decision to leave her little girl behind. It didn't matter that they needed to leave the area as fast as possible.

From here, he could keep them off the main roads and away from the search that would ensue. None of it mattered as much as the pain he heard next to him. He swung the car onto a dirt road, yanked the keys and jumped outside.

Right this minute, Alicia needed him as a friend,

someone to hold her as she grieved. He'd never comforted a civilian before. It would be a new experience for him, but it was necessary. They weren't exactly touchy-feely in the navy. He'd compensate his lack of know-how with sheer willpower to take whatever she dished out without a negative response. Surely she'd get it together before he needed to say anything. Right?

Hoping any effort from him would help her, he opened the door, knelt awkwardly with a knee on the floorboard and pulled her into his arms. She resisted at first, grabbing the steering wheel with one hand and the seat belt with the other. When his strength won out, she collapsed against his chest.

"I don't want you to touch me," she said as her arms contradicted her, landing on either side of his neck. "Oh, God, Johnny. How could you let this happen?"

The words she muttered changed to giant sobs. He just held her. None of her dislike of how he'd handled the extraction mattered. The physical stress mixed with the emotional upheaval of the past few days. She just needed someone to hang on to. And he was her only choice.

As her crying shuddered through her body, the strain tightened his muscles. He held her closer, skintight to keep her from breaking free. His jaw cracked with his own apprehension. If he had done something differently, would Alicia be holding Lauren instead of him?

Did she believe the failed rescue was his fault? She didn't really want an answer about how it had happened. Right? He could provide it. He'd written a hundred reports answering the hard question of how the best-planned op had detoured into a nightmare.

He didn't know what to say—if he should say anything at all. He'd never dealt with failure in a good way. It didn't sit well in his gut. But other botched operations didn't hold a candle to this one. Her crying shuddered to a stop as she pounded on his shoulder. She continued to chant, "Why, why, why," again and again. He could always push the doubt aside and eventually lock the memories in a place they didn't surface.

Very few ever involved children.

Not this. Not Alicia.

Someone as caring and giving as she was deserved to be protected, pampered. Deserved something to go right in her life. There was a long list of how he'd underestimated his opponent tonight. Another list of what he'd done wrong afterward. But there was only one promise he could make.

"No matter what it takes." No matter what it cost him—family or career. He'd give anything and everything. "I'll reunite you with your daughter."

She drew a deep, shuddering breath and tilted

her questioning eyes in wonder at him. Instead of wanting to gently set her away and get back on the road, he wanted to keep her tucked close or kiss her into oblivion.

Damn it to hell, he was falling in love with her all over again.

Chapter Sixteen

Straighten up and fly right. Her dad's phrase from one of his favorite songs.

Why the words were in Alicia's mind at this particular moment, she had no idea. Was she ready to sit straight and stop lamenting over what had happened?

But John had left her child in the hands of murderers. Could she forgive him long enough to accept his help? She had to. She had no choice. She would rescue her daughter no matter what it took. *No matter what it took.* That was her answer.

It was time to leave the protection of his strong arms wrapped securely around her and determine what they needed to do next.

"You okay now?" he asked. The phone vibrated on the console.

"No. But I'll function." She tapped his shoulders, hoping he'd release her before she lost it again. "It's probably Devlin with news. You need to answer it."

"We have a lot of work ahead of us, you know."

He stood, sweeping the phone into his hand at the same time. "Yeah?"

John walked to the front of the car and finished his conversation. The serious look on his face didn't really indicate whether the news was good or bad. The look was almost always there. She couldn't remember anything he'd asked Devlin or Brian to do before they'd gotten to the kidnappers' house. She'd been focused on following Patrick, on getting Lauren away from the monsters who had stolen her. She hadn't been listening to John's plans or if she'd been included.

Since this debacle had begun, he'd been multitasking, thinking ahead, planning the next move. Totally unlike the young recruit who had graduated from high school and left for boot camp without any plans to return. She'd admitted he'd changed.

So had she.

She'd become an adult, so it was logical that John had done the same. Gone were the boyish grin and the never-grow-up attitude. Replaced by a complete and focused concentration, along with a speak-when-spoken-to response.

She could handle that. Maybe. She wasn't as completely immune to the attraction between them as he seemed to be. Lying under him, even in a dangerous situation like minutes before, she'd found it hard not to remember the lean, sinewy muscles his body had developed. If he had any response to her, he hid it well.

Even when being in his arms gave her comfort, he seemed to pull back the passion. With one exception—their kiss in front of Joe. Both times she'd kissed him had jump-started her heart in a way she hadn't thought would ever be possible again after Dwayne died.

But she wasn't ready. There was too much chaos in her life, too many problems with no foreseeable solutions.

No matter what happened with her, John would leave anyway. He was here to help save his brother and Lauren. And when J.W. was better, he'd return to his mysterious assignments protecting the world. He'd never be satisfied pinned down with a family in their little country corner.

No, she was far from ready to fall for anyone. Especially him.

Don't read anything into those hugs other than their intent to keep you from falling completely apart. She was a soldier to him. Someone who needed to accomplish his goal. Nothing more. Nothing less.

John got back in the car in silence, turned it around and headed northeast—the opposite direction from the lake where Devlin was staying. She didn't mind a change in plans, but being included in the discussion every once in a while would be nice.

Who was she kidding? She had no experience and would follow his instructions and advice. She understood her limited role. And at the back of her mind there was the question of whether he'd dump her someplace safe to get her out of his hair. She needed to be mature, gain control of her emotions and be helpful. A faithful sidekick, not a hindering fool who screwed things up.

"Where are we going?"

"Dev checked the scanners. We're avoiding the police. Looks like the cops received a call from the Webers earlier, saying they'd been contacted by the kidnappers and had chosen to deliver the ransom themselves. By the time the police got to the ransom-exchange address, Patrick supposedly would have Lauren back."

"So they staged the entire event to make themselves look like heroes. But we interrupted and reinforced their claim that I was behind the abduction. I'm sorry I messed everything up."

"How do you figure that?" he asked, his voice deep and quiet.

"I couldn't sit in the car and wait. I thought you should know there was a second car. I thought Patrick had an accomplice who would get the jump on you or something. So I tried to warn you."

"I get that."

"Did Patrick plan to kill Tory before we showed up? Or was she killed because of me?" she asked, full of guilt that her presence may have caused the young woman's death.

John rubbed his free hand across his mouth and jaw stubble. Contemplating something. "Tell me about Patrick and Shauna."

"Like what?" He'd avoided her question, but she wouldn't forget to ask it again. She wanted to know the truth and take responsibility. Had Patrick hired Tory and her boyfriend to handle the kidnapping? If he had, then why had he brought a gun to pick up her daughter? It didn't make sense.

"For starters, did you think Weber was capable of shooting anyone?" John draped his wrist over the top of the wheel. Casual. Relaxed. Yet there was a tension in the way he sat and the way he constantly searched the mirrors.

"No. I'm still having a hard time absorbing it. You don't think it was an accident or that he was aiming at you? I mean, he knew Tory from Lauren's day care."

They were in the middle of nowhere. Illuminated only by the dashboard lights, John's face was all sharp angles and serious glare. Either deep in thought or terribly irritated. She couldn't tell. Either way she had a strange feeling she wouldn't like what he was about to say.

"Alicia." He pulled to a stop sign and faced her. "Weber didn't hesitate to shoot that woman, and he did it with Lauren on his hip."

"What does that mean?"

"I think he's done it before and had gone there with the intention of killing the two witnesses to the actual kidnapping. Then there'd only be Lauren, who would sound confused since she knew Tory from her school."

"Oh, my gosh. Who do you think he's killed before today?" Fear clogged her throat, but she swallowed the lump and pushed it away. She could be scared later, when she was alone. Not now. Now she had to help get her little girl back. Who could it have been? A slow realization filled her. "You think he killed Roy Adams."

"It's a logical assumption. Dwayne was…gone. If Roy was dead, Shauna would inherit. Did she know about Lauren's trust fund receiving the bulk of the money?"

"No. I mean, I don't think so. I didn't know about it either, honestly. Roy probably changed his will after Dwayne died."

"Where was his body found, again?" His free hand rubbed his chin in thought. It softened his chiseled features.

"At the old barn Joe told us about."

"Why was he out there when the stables are nowhere nearby?"

She shook her head. "I'm sorry, John, but I really don't know. I was sort of in a daze after Dwayne's accident. Lauren was six months old. I had to put

Dad in a full-care facility. And Roy convinced me
to move back to his house. Shauna hated that, of
course. I moved to Denton a couple of months later
when I went back to work full-time. It made more
sense to live closer to the hospital."

"You didn't see any signs?"

"As in signs of depression? No. I didn't see him
as often after we moved. Roy seemed preoccupied.
But Shauna made the town aware she'd been hiding his depression from everyone, especially me."

"But you don't think he committed suicide?"

"At the time? I didn't want to believe it could
happen to someone so close to me, but it's what
the authorities concluded. I didn't know to question their decision."

More than anything, she'd felt betrayed by the
last person who'd given her emotional support. A
very selfish thought to have. And then the guilt
had hit her. She was a health-care professional, and
several people had asked how she'd missed his depression. They'd almost accused her of being responsible.

"And what about now?" John asked.

"After Shauna and Patrick have kidnapped Lauren and killed Tory? I think Roy's *suicide* was very
convenient." She wanted to confront them both
and demand the truth. "It also makes me wonder
if Dwayne actually had an accident. Roy questioned
it all the time."

John shoved the car in gear, putting on a little too much gas, fishtailing a bit as the tires left gravel and connected with pavement. He hit the dashboard and then searched for the cell he'd tossed on the console.

"What's wrong?" She placed the phone in his hand so he could keep his eyes on the road. "I can help, if you let me."

"You should have said something." He tapped the breaks to slow down.

"Told you what, John? I don't understand."

"People are dropping around you like flies, woman. Haven't you noticed?"

"Noticed?" The shaky breath she managed to pull in barely stayed the tears of hurt from cascading down her cheeks. Hurt or fright? "I've done more than *notice* the ones I've loved leaving me. I've lived it. You can't possibly think Patrick and Shauna killed them both?"

John stared at her so long, she thought he might have forgotten he was driving the car. He got that look on his face. Troubled. Hurting. Haunted. The same things she felt deep down, especially when she was alone.

"I think there's something in that barn. Or there was. Something to make your father-in-law become preoccupied and stop seeing you and his grandchild. There's no other reason for Roy to hang out there like you said he was doing."

"Will knowing help get Lauren back?"

"We have to do more than get your daughter back, Alicia. Only the truth will get your and Brian's lives back. It's all connected. We just have to determine how and prove it."

"I can't believe I missed all this. You've been home less than a week and have uncovered so much. If I hadn't been caught up in my own little world of problems, I would have—"

"Stop beating yourself up. No one else noticed, either. No one had a reason to notice or suspect foul play. If there's one thing I've learned during twelve years of deployment around the world—" John paused, visibly swallowed hard "—evil has a habit of disguising itself to get whatever it wants."

The cold authority in his voice sent a chill down Alicia's spine.

Chapter Seventeen

It was a clear night, and the moon provided enough light to see through the open field and the overgrown path to Roy's barn. John cut the car's lights when he left the road. Each bumpy lurch of the small car felt like crossing a gully—lots of bumps as a result of nonuse. He wouldn't have cared if he hadn't spent the past two hours driving in circles, waiting for Alicia to fall into an exhausted slumber.

He pulled the rental slowly through the forgotten alfalfa and weeds on the far side of the run-down barn. Run-down, but he noticed a fairly new air-conditioning unit added crookedly in the middle of the wall. Odd, since units like that normally fit into windows. Whatever Roy had been doing out here either had been moved somewhere else, or no one felt it important, since it was obvious no one had kept this property maintained since his death.

The phone vibrated in his lap. He ignored it as he had the three times before. He hadn't answered it, fearing even his voice would wake Alicia. She'd been pushed to her limit. Everything had been taken from her and if she didn't get some rest, he wasn't sure how she'd react the next time something happened.

And the way his luck had been running, it—whatever *it* was—would definitely go wrong and happen. Military ops coordinated from halfway around the world seemed a lot easier than dealing with the unpredictable rationale of civilians.

Leaving the military would be a huge change. An idea that he was getting more comfortable accepting.

He parked the car and got out without jarring the vehicle too much. The inside bulb was still taped over, so no light shone on his sleeping beauty. He jogged out of earshot and answered the vibrating cell. "Yeah?"

"Where the hell have you been?" His brother sounded loud without raising his voice. Somehow he'd always been able to do that.

Then again, Brian's voice hadn't only come through the cell. He spun around and was face-to-face with his short-haired twin.

"When I texted where we were going, I didn't expect you to meet us here. You weren't followed?" Inadequacy reared its ugly head as John searched for the car he'd missed or additional cars on the horizon.

"I came on horseback." Brian threw a thumb

toward the south end of the barn, indicating where he'd left the animal. "The deputy assigned to me is parked on the road, probably sound asleep by now. It's not my first time avoiding a tail."

Brian shoved saddlebags into his chest with an extra push that forced John back a step. His twin wasn't elaborating on "avoiding a tail," and as much as he wanted to ask about the past twelve years, he couldn't. He had other things to worry about.

"There was no way I was going to let Mabel get any more involved by bringing you food." Brian continued moving. He was always moving, never seeming to relax around him at all. "Which she insisted you'd need by now."

"Thanks. She was right, but you shouldn't be here." His words sounded as forced as they felt. Maybe he was as *unrelaxed* around Brian as it seemed his *big* brother was around him.

"Grow up." Brian threw his hands above his head and turned to walk to his tethered horse. "Did you expect Mabel to come?"

"I didn't ask for any food and I didn't ask for your help."

"But you got it anyway, didn't you?" He spun on his booted toe. "You're back three days and you manage to drag Dad and Mabel into a dangerous situation right along with you. We're all supposed to just chip in, follow your orders and lie through our teeth so you can play the big badass navy SEAL coming to the rescue."

"What does that mean?" He hadn't asked to become involved in the kidnapping. There wasn't any way to explain that to free his brother he'd had no choice but to get involved.

Brian threw his hands lamely in the air. "Forget it. We're all in this up to our necks now. You've got no right to keep us in the dark."

"Us? Meaning you. Why? How did *you* plan to rescue Alicia? I seem to remember you were in jail and she was headed there." The old Brian would never believe the deciding factor to leave Dad and jump into this fray was to clear Brian's name. It hadn't happened twelve years ago, so why would the selfish brother do it now? Right? At this exact moment he didn't really know the answer to that question, either.

"I don't know, but I wouldn't have put Dad and Mabel at risk of landing there, too." Brian scratched his freshly shorn head and pressed his lips together as if he wanted to say something, but he wouldn't. "Dammit, I probably would've done the same thing. It's not like you had much choice."

"I can tell it hurt to admit that." It had always been hard for him to admit Brian was right, and he hadn't enjoyed the experience. He should confess, too. One more minute to enjoy this moment. Involving them had been a tough on-the-spot decision. It had been his only choice, but that didn't make it the right one.

Brian paced liked a caged animal. The area was six square feet. The same size as a jail cell. Something more was bothering his brother. Bothered him, too. They needed to talk. It just wasn't the right time.

Would it ever be? Not really.

"I didn't pick this fight," he admitted. It was the best he could do.

"You're saying you aren't responsible for dragging us into this mess?" Brian asked through clenched teeth, his hands balled into fists.

"I couldn't let Alicia go to jail." *And can't admit that wasn't the only reason you became involved.*

"But letting me go there was just fine. Of course, I should be used to that by now. Right?"

"So we're back to the fire? Well, going to jail while they investigated was your choice back then, since I didn't need defending. I didn't do anything."

"Forget it. That subject is dead. Buried." Brian looked around him, through him, but not *at* him. He didn't meet his eyes, but he didn't walk away.

"Not quite buried. More like a zombie that rises at every occasion. Sure doesn't seem dead."

"There's nothing left to talk about."

"How about the truth?" Maybe now was the right time to talk about it after all? "I fought with Alicia. She caught a ride before I could catch her.

The party broke up. I looked around and our truck was gone. I put the fire out and walked to the old clubhouse."

"You must have done a half-ass job putting it out, since the barn burned to the ground. I knew you were drunk, and shouldn't have let Dwayne talk me out of dragging you home."

His brother spoke with such venom and resentment. Had he been feeling that way the entire twelve years or had the hatred been gaining ground with each year they'd been separated? Was it anger that had kept him from coming home to face Brian? Not recently. But a long time ago, he'd been pretty mad.

"That's the thing, Brian. I wasn't drunk. I saw you with Alicia. *You* were the one completely wasted that night. We argued after you made a play for my girl and I didn't believe Alicia when she said nothing happened."

"You're crazy. I wouldn't do that. Besides, Dwayne took me home." The pacing stopped. Brian stood, grinding a fist into his palm. Ready to fight. Maybe even subconsciously inviting a fight.

John's fist twitched, responding, until he forced his fingers open. He just shook his head. "That story's full of holes. I'm telling you, the truck was gone. I walked and wasn't drunk."

"If you didn't leave the fire going, then who went back? They had a witness who saw our truck there.

Why lie about what happened, Johnny? You trying to convince Alicia you're worthy of her? Better wait until she's actually around."

His brother really believed the dribble he spouted. Even under moonlight, John could see the sincerity and confidence. Two minutes ago he'd been tired, worn-out and wanting to avoid another confrontation. The itch to fight and settle this once and for all was there, and no matter how exhausted he'd been, adrenaline kicked him into full gear.

Throughout their childhood and high school years they'd settled their differences with a fight. Rolling on the ground, punching kidneys, ripping shirts and jeans along the way. Why should now be any different? It had just taken twelve years to have it out about this one.

Without thinking too much about it, he rammed a sore shoulder into Brian's gut and they tumbled to the ground. Brian landed a hard fist in his side. Already bruised from Gargantuan's punches, John yelled in pain.

"Admit that you left the fire burning," Brian shouted, throwing another punch that rattled John's teeth.

"Admit that you felt guilty about making a play for Alicia and never gave me the chance to tell you the truth." John threw his own fist to crack Brian's jaw, then clamped his mouth shut to stop the groan of pain he wanted to release. His knuckles and lots of other body parts were already raw due to his earlier brawl.

They rolled in a deadlock, equally matched and equally tired. Brian groaned after a flip to his back when John landed a knee close to his groin. Then they reversed and broke apart as he narrowly avoided a furious knee slamming onto his chest.

He locked his arm behind Brian's head but couldn't finish the defensive move without snapping his brother's neck. He needed a minute to catch his breath and decide where to go. In the past, the victor had won the argument. Problem solved. But winning wouldn't resolve this ongoing problem between them.

Finding out the truth would.

"Well, it's about time." A very feminine voice laughed.

John looked upside down into Alicia's gorgeous smile as she bent over them. She didn't appear mad at all.

They both relaxed their grips just like they'd been caught fighting by their mother all those years ago. They rolled off one another and scrambled to their feet. He expected Alicia to scold them for being stupid. Instead she stretched open her arms, running to them and pulling them into an embrace.

"How much did you hear?" John asked over her shoulder.

"Did you really expect me to stay asleep with the two of you yelling at each other?"

John's eyes connected with his twin's, reflecting the shock he felt. Alicia's face was buried between them but he thought she muttered something about waiting a long time for this fight to clear the air.

"Wait a minute," Brian said, pulling back from the awkward group hug. "I wouldn't say anything's been cleared up." He wiped the blood from his lip with the back of his hand.

"I agree." John set Alicia slightly away from him, half expecting her to stomp her foot in frustration.

John edged his tongue across his own lip, itching to wipe the wetness away, not ready to admit Brian had drawn blood.

"But you're finally fighting it out. If you'd done this that night, we could have avoided the strained relationships and years of hurt."

Brian backed farther away. "Nothing would have changed, Alicia. He was a jerk of a kid, always avoiding getting blamed for anything."

"Is that what you think? You've really believed I was guilty all these years? You think I was drunk and irresponsible. That I set the fire and couldn't face the truth?"

"I think I'll wait in the barn." Brian darted around the building.

"Oh, no, you don't, Brian Sloane." Alicia did

stomp her foot and shout. Brian returned as far as the corner and leaned against the aging wall. "You two are going to get this over with, even if it requires a broken nose." She pointed her finger at him, then back around at Brian. "Or two. Now get on with it."

"There's nothing to argue about," his brother said, visibly clenching his jaw and swallowing hard. "He won't admit he was there."

Watching his twin, he realized just how much their gestures revealed. He was bone weary and emotionally done and Brian didn't look much better. He was holding his right ribs—not the left, where John's fist had connected several times. Somebody left-handed had taken some shots.

Alicia looked expectantly at him to start the reconciliation. He stuck his hand out in front of him and shrugged. "What do you want me to say? I wasn't."

"Well, let's start with who drove the truck home that night. It wasn't me. I rode home with Trina Kaufman. Or I drove her home listening to her snores." Alicia put her hands on her hips, forcing Brian not to turn away. She flicked a finger and he responded like a little kid, shuffling forward, back within arm's distance.

Do I look like that?

Was that a bit of courage straightening his own

spine? This slip of a woman, in spite of all the problems she'd faced, would be the driving force behind resolving the feud with his brother. She had courage and stamina worthy of any navy SEAL. He should be ashamed it had come to this, but in a way, he was relieved.

For better or worse, the time had come to clear the air.

"It doesn't sound like either of us drove Granddad's truck home," he said, drawing on the courage to see the conversation through without throwing another punch. "I was in the tree house."

"I stayed at Dwayne's," Brian mumbled.

Realization hit John about the same time as Brian. Neither of them was responsible for the fire. Twelve years of anger could have been avoided.

"So neither of you drove the truck home. But there were witnesses who saw the truck leaving Mrs. Cook's after the fire started."

"Son of a bitch." Brian turned away from Alicia with a string of curses and a fist slamming the rotten barn wall. "Anyone could have taken the truck. We always left the keys in it at those things since we shared it. Everybody knew that. I mean, we never thought anyone would steal it."

"Someone framed us good enough that even *we* bought the story." John wanted to punch something through the barn wall. He settled for slamming his fist into his palm.

"And since you never asked each other," Alicia continued, "you just assumed the other was responsible."

"Yeah. We were idiots and have paid the price for our stupidity," Brian admitted for them both.

"Twelve years." Alicia's body relaxed. Her arms went above her head and smoothed her curly hair, pulling it into a ponytail and twisting it into a knot. "Twelve frustrating years of silence when a two-minute conversation would have resolved everything. Men."

The soothing gesture hit him somewhere between his heart and lower regions. Sexy, natural, pleasing. It was all of the things he wanted but seemed far out of his reach.

He heard the cell vibrating in the dirt where he'd dropped it during the scuffle with Brian. His brother plopped easily on the ground to sit and answered it as he scooped it up. Speaker on, it was flat in his brother's palm before John could object.

"Sloane, cop scanner has them heading for this place. Somebody must have reported seeing you here. I'm taking a few essentials and packing out since you took my rental and your vehicle seems compromised." Devlin's stressed voice filled the awkward silence.

"Sorry, man."

"It'll take me a half hour to trek this stuff to another car. Where we meeting up?"

"That location I had you checking out. We're there now."

"Roger. Gotta run. Literally."

The line disconnected and Brian held out the phone. John grabbed it, shoving the thing in his back pocket. He checked his lower back. No weapon—not in the dirt anywhere. Man, he'd left it in the car. What was wrong with him?

His brother stretched and yawned. Relaxed. Really relaxed and comfortable. He touched his forehead and then shoved his hand across the high and tight haircut. "Dammit, I hate short hair. Top of my head'll be sunburned for sure first time I feed the horses."

"Tell me about it." He scratched his own scruff, noticing they now had the same exact cut. "I've lost my cover a time or two in training. Sunburn up top is the worst."

Mabel would make a great military barber.

"Well, not the worst. I remember your mother talking about you two skinny-dipping one summer," Alicia dropped casually as she picked up the saddlebags. "Didn't you both fall asleep without any clothes?"

They all burst out laughing. That had been a miserable week spent sitting in alcohol and oatmeal baths. "At least when we fell asleep we were in the shade and not trying to lose our tan lines."

"Oh, my gosh, the burn I got that summer was horrible." Alicia protectively covered her breasts.

He remembered the miserable couple of days she'd walked around braless. Just as miserable for him and his imagination as for her and her sunburned flesh.

"Both of us were sicker than dogs," Brian said, still on the ground, one arm draped over a bent knee. "What now?"

He wished he knew. John was surprised his brother had asked the question instead of Alicia. But at a glance he knew she'd wanted to. It was in her eyes, along with the worry and fright concerning the unknown. Still there. She might smile and laugh, but it was still there.

"I, for one, am hoping there's food in those saddlebags." She headed for the hand-tooled leather.

Brian nodded. "Mabel sent something. I threw in a change of clothes. My old boots are still on my saddle. Just in case you need to go into town impersonating me. Not many people look my direction or talk much to me, so you won't need to get up-to-date on my life or anything to keep up," he added with an unfamiliar smirk.

"I'll keep that in mind."

"And never smile. Brian never, ever smiles when he's in town," Alicia teased.

"Right."

What was the tension he was picking up between

these two? Was it real? Or just a continuation of the night of the fire? She'd told him that what he'd seen had all been a joke. A simple dare from Brian's friends. He hadn't found it that funny, and they'd argued. Then they'd broken up afterward because of him not believing her.

At least he thought they had. They must have. Great. He felt like he was eighteen again. Confused emotions and a growing ache for Alicia that just wouldn't stop—no matter who was around or what danger they were in.

He wanted to pull her close to him. Her arms were still above her head, so they'd fall on his shoulders and her breasts would end up flush with his chest. The image of her next to him was so clear in his mind, he shook his head to get rid of it.

When he opened his eyes, she stood close in front of him, a perplexed wrinkle between her brows. But Brian…he had a knowing look. An "I told you so" laugh that turned into a short approving whistle.

"Where were you just now?" Alicia asked, still searching his face with questioning dark blue eyes.

"Yeah, brother dearest, where were you?"

Brian knew exactly where he'd been. No doubt about it. Behind Alicia's back he spotted his brother mouthing, *It's about damn time.* The momentary panic trying to creep up his spine was just confusion at his brother's perceptive grin. His twin seemed…almost happy at the prospect he was having thoughts about Alicia. Didn't his brother want her for himself?

Brian shook his head and muttered, "You're still an idiot."

"You're both idiots and we're wasting time," Alicia said, turning from John to face Brian, with a bit of apple between her lips. "You're no better than he is, you know. By the way, I'm sorry you went to jail because of me."

"No big deal."

"It's always a big deal." She dragged a finger across Brian's jaw. "That's not from your scuffle with John. Sure wish we had a frozen bag of peas to put on it. I really am sorry."

Brian's gaze connected with his and he took a quick couple of steps away from Alicia. If his brother could read him, he was definitely picking up on the instant jealousy that had taken over with an instant thought that had popped in his head.

Mine!

Her sympathy should be directed at him. John. *He* was the one who had the crap beat out of him by a giant while trying to unsuccessfully rescue her child.

Get past it. She isn't yours. She's with you because she has no other choice. Just move on and find her daughter. Then you can get the hell away from her and whatever this possessiveness is all about.

Right. Past her. Past the feeling of wanting someone who was much too good for him. He didn't deserve anyone as special as Alicia Adams. He knew it even if no one else did.

Chapter Eighteen

"What are we going to do now?" Shauna screeched as soon as the housekeeper had taken Lauren upstairs.

Break your neck so the endless screeching will stop. The situation was heartbreaking to only himself, but Patrick admitted he'd have to endure several weeks of screeching before it would ever stop. But he could dream.

The brat had screamed and cried for her mother every minute after the police escort to the station. She'd shut up as soon as he'd reminded her of what had happened to her babysitter. In fact, she hadn't uttered a word after he'd whispered in her ear. He wished the same could be said for Shauna.

Patrick watched his hysterical wife frantically twist a strand of the red frizz she took an hour to straighten every time she saw it in a mirror. He hated her hair. Almost as much as he hated her. The dyed color was purple in fluorescent light, nowhere near the red on the box. He knew only because she'd ranted for days and days that they should sue the hair-color company.

In his sad, wimpy way, he'd agreed with her until she'd moved on to the next threat of a lawsuit and rant.

Tory had had lovely hair.

He sat on the end of the couch and flipped up the built-in footrest. "You've got the kid, dear. Isn't that what you wanted?"

He yawned. As soon as his head hit the pillow, he'd sleep like a hibernating bear. He opened his mouth to suggest they head upstairs. Then reconsidered. He knew his partner in crime needed to spout her concerns out loud and he didn't want the housekeeper hearing her.

I wonder if I could slip a sleeping pill into her drink? Or two or three?

She'd pass out on the couch and he'd have the bed to himself, minus the stench of her night creams and moisturizers.

No. If he did, she would oversleep in the morning and the complaining would be worse. Tomorrow was an early one. Lots of bathroom prep for the camera attention she craved.

"The police suspect something. I know they do." Shauna poured herself a two-finger drink of his good scotch and shot it back easier than water.

"Keep your voice down. As long as you don't talk about it, they won't have any idea we're behind everything." *Same as you have no idea I've been pulling all the strings for years.* He sat forward, no longer relaxed, needing to be alert to keep her calm. "You heard them at the station. They issued a warrant for Alicia."

She slammed the glass down on the bar. "But not Brian. He was there. You saw him sitting under your girlfriend. That bitch, Mabel, is lying for him."

"Why does it matter so much? It's Alicia you want destroyed, right?"

She twisted more of her straw-like hair. Then pulled at the bottom of her shirt. She'd freak out when she realized that the kid had gotten dirt all over the frilly white thing Shauna had worn. His wife had wanted to be photographed in the see-through blouse after they'd "rescued" Lauren.

Everything was about appearances and the money. *Nothing wrong with money as long as you have plenty of it.* Even Tory had been all about the money. More of it. Every question had been about the money and how they were going to use it to get to Paris.

Well, he'd been to Paris and had no desire to go back. The money would last longer on a beach in Mexico, and that was where he was headed as soon as this crap was done. The kid would officially be in their custody and shipped off to a boarding school. God, how long would *that* take?

Shauna would come with him, of course. He

already had her careful scrawling signature down pat. So he wouldn't have to put up with her too long while he transferred all the money to himself.

Once she's gone...heaven.

"Are you listening to me?"

"Of course I am, sweetheart." *Not really. My fantasies are much better company.*

He was lucky he didn't choke on the endearment. He'd transfer the money as fast as he could and would savor choking her scrawny neck. He had dreamed about it several times and would have all the details planned. He'd insist they rent a sailboat, small enough he could manage it on his own. Even now he could envision her tanned skin in one of those bright white string bikinis she liked to wear. He'd bring her a drink—something fruity so she'd sip it slowly. She'd sit up on her towel; he'd offer to put more lotion on her back to keep her from burning.

Then he'd slip his fingers gently across her larynx and tighten his grip. She starved herself all the time, so she'd be unable to fight back. Weak, she had no strength. Not like him.

Wait, that wouldn't do. If he was behind her, he couldn't see her eyes bulge and then go dead. Forget the drink. He'd untie the strings and make her think he wanted sex on the deck. Maybe he'd have her one last time before squeezing the breath from her and cracking her spine.

He'd always wanted to snap a spine. Had always been curious if you could really hear the pop like the sound effects they used in the movies and on television. Would it be as easy? Did it require practice? It wouldn't hurt to practice. Maybe he'd get a chance once or twice before the sailing excursion.

"What are you smiling at?"

Her whispered shout drug him back to reality.

"You, darling." He deliberately smiled bigger at her. If it irritated her, he just had to continue.

"There's nothing to smile about," she droned on. "It's obvious she's hired help. I have no idea where she got any money. Probably from that drug-dealer boyfriend of hers."

So they were still discussing how Brian Sloane could be sitting at the Aubrey Diner counter and not lying on the ground under Tory. He'd almost hated to pull the trigger and end that scene. She'd been clawing at him and he hadn't punched her once. The sheer strength in the man's hands was admirable. And deadly. A true killer in the making. *Or breaking.*

He'd never noticed that about Brian before. And the new haircut... Why had he shorn his head?

"You know there's another possibility of how Brian could be in two places at the same time." Why hadn't he reasoned it out before?

"What are you blathering about?" She crossed her arms under her tiny breasts.

Tory had a terrific stack up top. *Had. Past tense.* "John. He's back. He probably returned the day your private detective took the picture. Think about it. We've waited weeks for Alicia to do something with Brian. But remember, love, she was always *John's* girlfriend."

"Oh, my God. That explains everything. We have to call the police." She made a beeline to the phone.

"There's no rush, honey. You can have an epiphany during your interview tomorrow."

They'd already been contacted by the local news stations. Shauna had given her cell number to all of them. She'd answered the questions during their initial conversation with the county sheriff, which had frustrated the man to no end. It was definitely laughable.

Playing the silent incompetent had quickly grown tiring. But he'd sat there, letting Shauna do all the talking. Seeming in control. It wouldn't be long now. Just a matter of days and he could stop acting. They'd sell the rest of the Adams property, have the cash in the bank, control of the kid's trust fund, and all the ties to his small-town past working in stalls ankle deep in horse manure would be broken.

"What if they snatch Lauren back? Or decide to kill us in our sleep?"

"That's being slightly dramatic, dear. If Sloane— no matter which one—wanted to kill us, I imagine he could have accomplished that easily tonight. I'm sure both of them have had enough practice with a gun not to miss. And whoever was there had every opportunity. The man restrained himself from hitting Tory when they were squirming on the ground together." He remembered the power of pulling the trigger and watching the blood spread across her blond hair. The ground had darkened as it pooled beneath the yellow halo.

Knowing that he'd been in control of Tory's life excited him. His only regret was not moving closer. Had she known she was dying? Or was shooting her in the head as instantaneous as they claimed?

Then again, the surprise on Sloane's face had been priceless. That was where he'd really been watching. If it had been John, why was he so affected by the measly death of a day-care worker? Hadn't he seen death hundreds of times over while in the military?

Shauna was wringing her hands again and reaching for the phone. "They could find that girl's boyfriend and force him to admit that we hired him. He's still missing, you know."

He wrapped her skinny fingers within his fists. "I couldn't take care of him tonight. John or Brian—whoever was helping Alicia—was fighting him when I walked out with the money." He kissed her fingertips instead of squeezing to demand she stop. "I'm sure Tory's boyfriend is getting as far away from Aubrey, Texas, as possible. And if not, I can convince him to work for us a bit longer."

"Why didn't you take care of them all? You said you would. That was the plan. You said it wouldn't be a problem for you to shoot them and make it look like self-defense."

God, she was tiresome. "Shauna, neither of us could predict that Alicia would find the kid. I still don't know how they did."

"They probably followed you, you fool." She jerked her fingers from his and circled the room where not four hours ago they'd gone over the plan while having a glass of wine to soothe her nerves.

"Why don't you have another drink before we head to bed, sweetheart?" He poured another scotch, hating to part with any drop of it, but knowing she'd pass out sooner if he did. "You'll have to look your best for the local talk shows tomorrow. Remember, darling, you're a hero."

Before handing her the drink, he faked a passionate kiss, pretending it was Tory pressed against him. She sipped and he let his hands caress her skin, drawing his thumbs across her protruding collarbone.

It would be so easy to be rid of his annoying problem.

All he'd have to do was squeeze.

Chapter Nineteen

"I sure hope the air conditioner works in there. Especially if we're stuck inside all day. It's going to be another scorcher." Alicia wiped the sweat from under her neck, leaving the men gawking at each other.

Joking about the good old days might smooth things over between John and Brian, but it was so long ago.... What kind of memory would her daughter have of this? How would she ever let Lauren out of her sight again? Kids getting sunburned on the banks of the creek didn't compare to your day-care teacher being shot in front of you by a person who you thought of as a grandparent.

Keep a lid on it. Don't fall apart or John will check you into the psych ward for observation.

Alicia could only stare at her shaking hands. In fact, there was a tremor throughout her entire body that wouldn't stop. She couldn't control the fright that was bubbling somewhere close to the fear that she'd never see her daughter again. She broke into a trot, heading in the direction John had parked.

God above, please keep my legs steady enough so I don't fall flat on my face.

She needed to be alone for a few minutes before diving into whatever had kept her father-in-law inside that barn. There was so much to take in that her mind went blank. Her only thought was to take one step at a time. Put her tennis shoe on the ground without turning her ankle and without tripping and falling. *One step. Another step.*

When she reached the car, she dropped her head against the cool metal of the roof, locked her knees in place and refused to cry.

"Don't lose it. You'll be okay." She'd chanted those words often enough in the past four years.

But she was far from okay. Tory was dead and her daughter had witnessed the woman's murder. Could she force herself to be in control? She'd done it before—she had to do it again. There wasn't a choice.

She turned around, leaning on the car and twisting her knotted hair into a tighter mess. It just took so much concentration to pretend. Constantly shoving the images of the night's events aside made her draw on a strength she hadn't used since Dwayne's funeral.

Her fingers were hot against her face as she scrubbed her eyes and held her breath for a moment. There was nothing there. Nothing left to draw from. After her husband's death, she'd replenished her empty heart by clinging to his daughter. And Roy had clung to them both.

What could she do? *Think of something else.*

The fight between Brian and John had taken her straight back to refereeing them in their teens. Even with all this stress, those happy days brought a smile. The brothers had bloody lips. She'd witnessed a restraint in John that had never been there in high school. He'd done his best to get the better of Brian back then.

Maybe he was as exhausted as she felt. Her short nap had only made her more tired. But it was more sleep than John had achieved. And she hadn't fought a giant of a man earlier or had an emotional encounter with her twin.

Nope, she'd just left her daughter in the hands of murderers. That was all she'd accomplished today. "Dear Lord." Her eyes burned with the hint of tears. *Focus on something else. You can't do this each time you think of Lauren.*

"You okay?"

At first glance, she thought John had followed her. The voice was the same. But Brian was close to her elbow, then patting her shoulder. Brian, her longtime friend.

"John's taking a look around. Hop in, I'm moving the car into the barn." He walked around the hood, the moon shining on his new "high and tight" haircut.

That was what John had called it in high school when Mabel had shorn his head with the ancient hair clippers his dad owned. "High and tight, Miss Mabel. Not one of those jarhead trims," he'd said.

She took a deep breath, wiped her eyes again and stood straight, then asked Brian, "Did he tell you what happened out there tonight?"

"The bare basics." He leaned on the roof opposite her. "I'm sorry."

"I really wish things were different, you know?" She slapped the car hard enough to make her hand sting. "Ow, darn it."

They both laughed—kind of. *So he feels just as weird as I do.*

"I made a pass at you the night of the fire, didn't I?"

"Yes."

"I pretended to be my brother for some reason. Right?"

"Yes. The guys dared you to find out if you and Johnny kissed the same, since you were physically identical."

"We wore the same jeans, boots and jackets that night? That's the reason no one knew which one of us left when. But you didn't need a kiss to know I wasn't him. How did you always know?"

"I'm not sure. But I've been able to tell you apart since the first day on the bus. You have two completely different attitudes about everything."

"I know. But that's not it. We can act like each other when we want to." He raised his brows, dipping his chin to his chest. The twins' longtime gesture to let her know that she was behind the curve.

"What do you think it is? Just tell me, please. Or do you really know?" Of course she was curious. She'd never been able to put her finger on the reason.

He tapped the hood with his finger a couple of times. Nothing dramatic, just a pause while he made up his mind. "I guess it's about time somebody set you two straight. Shoot. John looks at you differently. Always has."

"Like how?"

"Alicia, honey, my brother's been in love with you since he laid eyes on your skinny chicken legs in sixth grade." He got in the car. "If you need to hit someone, I recommend John."

She followed to the driver's side and bent to the open window. "I'm not going to hit you. I hardly believe a word out of your mouth." She laughed. On purpose, to cover her nervousness that Brian might actually be right. "Let him know I need a minute to think. That's why I came out here."

"I overheard Mom talking to Dad about it once. Way back in junior high, she told him you'd make a good daughter-in-law someday."

"There is no way on God's green earth that John Sloane has always been in love with me. We're friends. Same as you and me." She playfully gave a soft shove to his shoulder. "Stop foolin' around, Brian. He left, for gosh sakes. Just joined the navy and never looked back."

A sadness turned his playfulness into a death shroud.

"Alicia?" He caught her hand, stopping her from walking away.

She searched the stars for the strength to face him. She knew he wasn't John. He was right; somehow even their touch was different to her. But his voice, combined with the same haircut, made it hard to remember. And there was something in the way he'd said her name and held her hand that tugged at her heart.

"Yes?" She didn't bend down. She couldn't take him feeling sorry for her. She'd start crying for certain and lose it again.

"Give him a chance, will ya?"

Brian released her, started the car and pulled away.

Give him a chance?

"To do what?" she asked the retreating car.

She watched Brian pull into the barn and John

shut the doors. Her legs wobbled under her, so she plopped to the hard, dry earth. *Give him a chance? A chance to keep her out of jail? A chance to rescue Lauren? A chance to save her life? A chance to break her heart again?*

Their time for chances had long passed. Twelve years ago the opportunity for *chances* had come and gone. Gone. Gone. Gone.

Chapter Twenty

Alicia had one objective, and that was to get her daughter back in her arms and keep her safe. Nothing else mattered. Nothing.

She leaned back and rested on her elbows, then lay down on the sun-shriveled stalks of Johnson grass, folding her arms under her head. She could tell herself over and over again that nothing else mattered. She could spell it with giant capital letters and try to believe she was telling herself the truth.

But she wasn't.

John mattered. The shock and hurt she'd seen in him. The way he'd held her. The way they'd kissed. Lord, was it just yesterday that they'd been at Roy's house and escaped the police chief by climbing into the tree?

"Good. Grief." So much had happened since John had come home. There was no way he loved her. No way. He couldn't. Could he?

"No way," she shouted to the stars. Brian had to be wrong. Either way, it didn't matter. Not now.

They all had one objective, and that was to get Lauren back.

A soft breeze blew the treetops at the edge of the field, but it was the sound of feet crunching the dying grass that made her jerk to a sitting position.

"Did Brian upset you? Are you all right? I heard you cry out and—" John said, out of breath. He must have sprinted from the barn door.

"Of course I am. I was just…just…" She couldn't tell him she'd been weighing what she valued and he'd come in the top two. She wasn't ready for that. "Were you watching me?"

The arch of his brows expressed an emphatic *duh* without uttering the word. Classic Sloane-twin look. Seeing it twice in ten minutes made her feel slightly inadequate to deal with him. He bent at the waist and leaned on his knees, clearly tired. Still dragging air into his lungs.

"Just how long has it been since you had sleep?"

"I don't need sleep."

"Nonsense. I bet Brian can handle things until Dev arrives. Whatever occupied Roy's attention can wait a couple of hours." She gathered her feet under her, but before she could push off the ground, John's hands spanned her waist and he lifted her skyward.

Her toes dangled, touching nothing except air. Instead of just letting her drop to the earth, he drew her chest to his and let her slide to a disappointing halt. She stayed there with her hands on his shoulders, his sneaking around to her back. "I go without sleep a lot in my line of work."

"I, um… But you… John?"

"What?" His lips were very close.

Too close. There was too much between them to just pick up where they'd left off before their argument at graduation. Darn Brian and his silly ideas about love. Did either of them even remember that horrible, public argument? Or remember that she'd loved and married another man?

Not if the way he's holding you is any indication.

"Did you want to ask me something?" he teased through a grin.

"You can let go of me now." She firmly tugged on his forearms. Nice, muscled with just the right amount of fuzz on them. As often as she'd been around the house with Brian, she'd never noticed that before.

It was basically the same body, and yet Brian walking around the house without his shirt made her feel like her brother was home. This one? Well, the body under her fingertips, the thighs snug to her thighs… The chest her breasts were flattened against caused every part of her to hum. And parts that had been asleep since Dwayne had gone began to stir awake.

John released her. Almost. At the last moment,

he spun her around, keeping her back to his front, his arm circling her waist again.

"What are you doing?"

"There's no hurry," he whispered in her ear. "And I have something to say."

She tugged at the vise grip around her middle. It didn't hurt, but he wasn't budging. "You can't tell me while you're looking at me?"

"Exactly."

No more. Oh, goodness, not a confession. *I'm not ready.*

"So hurry up, then. Brian's waiting."

"Right." He shifted, taking her with him. Facing the edge of the field instead of the shaft of light peeking beneath the double barn door.

"We aren't kids anymore, Johnny. You can let me go. I won't run away. You're a grown man and should be able to say what you want. You do realize that we're both thirty. Adults, right? And that I'll listen to whatever you have to say?"

"The thing is, Alicia, I don't think I can honestly look at you when you answer. I need to know something before we go any further, and now's as good a time as later to finish the conversation." His hold on her relaxed and his hand trembled. "I understand if you thought I'd set the fire all those years. But can you believe me now? Do you believe me?"

He's afraid?

Looking at the treetops and the sinking moon was much easier than the temptation of his handsome face. So she stayed. Encircled by his arms, feeling safe. Filling her heart so she could go forward.

"At first, I didn't think either one of you could have done it. And thought it had been an accident even when Brian said he thought he'd put the fire out and other accusations flew around town. Life went on." Her voice didn't sound rattled any longer. "Until Dwayne died and Brian started coming around to help out, we never talked about it. When he told me that you'd been drunk and must have left the fire going, well, I didn't believe it but couldn't tell him why."

"Why?" His voice was soft and warm against her neck.

"It was your story to tell. I couldn't put a bandage on the wound you caused each other."

She suddenly wanted to kiss him and be kissed by him. Maybe it was better they weren't facing each other. Because if she started, she wouldn't want to stop. When he kissed her, she forgot the rest of the world and what was happening in it.

Lauren was too important. *Get her back, then worry about kissing Johnny Sloane!*

"Thing is, no one at the party would have left that fire going. Especially you and Brian. I've said that since the day you left."

JOHN'S BODY ACHED.

In training, he'd taken more brutal beatings than what Brian had dished out. For some reason this one had hit him hard. And then there was the fact that he was holding Alicia. He bent close enough that the hot summer breeze blew her hair against his cheek. He didn't want to move away, so he widened his stance, straining his already exhausted legs.

Alicia had never doubted his innocence. Nothing to worry about after all. Unlike his brother, who had jumped to a guilty verdict before ever talking to him. But he'd acted guilty by running off. He could admit that.

All his earlier resolve to blame his brother faded like a cloud covering the moon. He knew it was there, but couldn't see it clearly anymore. Believing John had been irresponsible, Brian had come rushing in to help again. Sure, he was full of blunder and guilt trips and better solutions, but bottom line? He knew his twin had his back.

They could trust each other again because of the woman in his arms. Probably a good thing they weren't face-to-face, since he wanted to kiss her till she couldn't think—among other things.

"Is that all you needed, John?"

"Needed?"

She rotated her body, negotiating the circle he'd created with his arms, letting his fingers drag around her waist. She lifted her left arm above him and skimmed just behind his ear with her finger. If she got much closer, she'd know exactly what he *needed*.

"Grass." She flicked something quickly away from them. "Must have been from the fight."

When her eyes tilted toward the heavens, they were nose to nose. Which also meant their mouths were just about on the same level, too. Alicia flicked her tongue across her bottom lip and rolled it between her teeth. He could feel his insides tightening at the thought of holding her even closer. It had been a long time, but he knew how soft her lips would become after he crushed them to his.

Not the spur-of-the-moment connections they'd achieved since he'd been home. He was remembering serious kissing. They'd both explored each other in a first kiss. He'd suffered through her years with braces. The scrapes on his lips had been worth it. In high school, they'd spent hours practicing everywhere. They'd joked about how kissing should be a game and kids could earn a high school letter jacket just like Brian had in every other sport.

How many times had he held her exactly the same way, not caring about the future? Dreaming of far-off places to explore—but only with her. That had changed after one argument and his stupid pride. Right here, right now, he just wanted her.

A future without her wasn't something he wanted to step into again.

His arms tightened, bringing her body flush with him. Sliding his fingers under her T-shirt, he connected with the flushed heat of her lower back. They were pretty much sharing the same space when his mouth devoured hers. Lips—slick and cool compared to the hot silkiness of her flesh under his fingertips. Soft and welcoming instead of contoured muscles, honed while working with patients.

Her body had changed, become more of everything good he remembered. He wanted her—it didn't matter if his brother was inside the barn or if Dev would be there any minute. He wanted to throw her over his shoulder and haul her to the far tree line so they wouldn't be found. They needed to be alone so she could cry out as much as she wanted. Or he could capture all her joy with his lips, savor it for the time they'd be apart.

The picture of her covered in perspiration as the moon shimmered over her naked flesh was vivid for him. He couldn't stop himself. He wanted more of her.

Their relationship had never been more than occasional young-love petting. Everyone thought they'd be the couple to get pregnant and forced to marry when they were sixteen, but it hadn't happened. Not that he hadn't wanted to, tried to, gotten elbowed in his gut a time or two.

"Johnny," Alicia said when he glided his lips along the V of her neck.

His thumbs skimmed the bottom curve of both breasts through the smooth satin of her bra. How many times had he fantasized about this moment? How many times had her face gotten him through a long night on a mission? Or through a long night rocking in his bunk, wondering what if they hadn't broken up?

"We have to…" Alicia sighed his name again and tipped her head back. "Oh, my."

He stopped thinking about teenage petting and dragged his thumb across the silky cup of lace. Her nipple immediately pebbled under the caress.

"We should… We can't."

"Why? Do you have a curfew?" he teased, stopping her questions with another long kiss. Tasting her unique combination of warm and cool and sweet.

His hand fully closed over her breast, and her hips surged into his. She knew exactly what he wanted. No doubt. He couldn't hide it. Her hand circled his wrist and gently tugged him away.

"No." Alicia's hands were planted firmly against his chest. Body contact lost.

John relaxed his hold, allowed her to step back. He should never have asked her a question or released her lips. They were adults, the only ones responsible for their actions.

"We can't do this—"

"You're right."

"You don't know what I'm about to say," she whispered, shaking her head.

"Yeah, I do."

She crossed her arms, tightly closed her mouth with a harrumph and shot him a look he couldn't really catalog. If Texas hadn't been in the middle of a triple-digit heat wave, the air would have frosted up as she stomped past.

She marched toward the barn, then did an about-face, sticking her finger in his face so close he could see her fingernail polish chipping.

"You have a lot of nerve coming back after twelve years and trying to pick up like nothing ever happened after you left."

He opened his mouth to apologize, but—

"No. Don't interrupt me. I'm finally going to say this without the fear you won't help me find Lauren." She closed her eyes, inhaled deeply and slapped her jeans. "I get it. You're a naval officer who probably has a gal in every port. Well, Lieutenant Sloane, my little part of the world doesn't have a dock. It's centered around a four-year-old child who has never had a father. I'm it. Her whole world. And I don't take risks with it. I loved Dwayne very much. It was real and something I'll never forget."

"I get it."

"No, I don't think you do. I have responsibilities to Lauren and have no intention of jeopardizing that by dating. Let alone having sex in a dried-up field with a man I haven't seen or heard from in over a decade."

"Don't worry about Lauren. We'll get her back. I'll call for the rest of my SEAL team if I have to." He forced a grin. "I understand, Alicia. Don't think anything about it."

"I don't want you to hate me."

Her hands shook. He noticed the tremor when she stroked his cheek before she walked briskly away. A smooth stroke down his jawline, just like she'd given Brian after their fight.

"Never." He'd never hate her. He'd never stay in this part of Texas. He'd never stop wanting her with every part of his being. *Never.*

His phone vibrated with a text. Slick. It was Brian, watching from the barn. Lights at the gate.

Probably Dev, but they couldn't be certain, and he'd been completely distracted by the beauty in his arms. *Damn!* He had to get this desire crap under control. If he didn't, he'd get them all thrown in jail. Or worse…dead.

Chapter Twenty-One

John hid the car Dev had "borrowed" at the back of the property in the far grove of trees he'd wanted to drag Alicia to just a short time ago. When he entered the barn, said woman was silent in the only chair, her forehead crinkled in thought while his best friend and brother held a discussion loud enough to be heard over the air conditioner.

He'd been gone only a few minutes, but it seemed they were all deep in contemplation. The men had parked themselves on either side of the rattling AC unit.

They all stared at the wrecked car that had belonged to Dwayne. The same car he'd crashed over four years ago, dried bloodstains on the tan seat. Nothing more of importance was inside the barn, other than hay for horses waiting in another paddock, to be sold at auction tomorrow.

His brother's thumbs were hooked in his belt loops as casually as his ankles were crossed while leaning against the barn wall. A big change from the way he'd paced like a caged animal an hour earlier. Dev's hand rested against his chin, one finger tapping across his lips.

John knew that look. The team knew to prepare for an onslaught of random brainstorming ideas until a workable solution was obtained. If they could reach that point and come up with a plan, he'd endure any number of questions from Dev.

"We're assuming Roy Adams came to this barn, probably turned on that clattering air conditioner, sat in that chair and what? Stared at the vehicle where his son died? Why?" Dev asked.

"And is answering that question worth our time before we figure out a plan to rescue Lauren?" Brian asked.

He didn't know.

"That's one mangled piece of junk." Dev half pointed with his tapping finger to the car they'd found. Hardly missing a beat, the tapping to his face resumed. "No drugs? No alcohol?"

"Toxicology screen was clean. Absolutely no alcohol in his system, man," Brian stated. "I'm telling you, he wasn't drunk. A friend of mine looked at the autopsy for me."

"You never mentioned you requested that, Brian," Alicia said softly. She looked straight ahead, through the missing driver's door of the car.

Brian shot John a plea for help, but there was no need. Dev's processing wouldn't be sidetracked.

"So they assumed he fell asleep," Dev mumbled, "but it wasn't late at night. Sort of a strange assumption, even for the cops."

"Shauna told everyone within earshot that he fell asleep at the wheel because he'd been up all night with Lauren."

"Had he?" Dev asked.

"Not more than usual. I worked all night and he was with her. He would have called if she hadn't been sleeping. She slept pretty soundly for a six-month-old. Still does."

There was a visible lack of emotion coming from Alicia. For a woman who had been so passionate less than twenty minutes before, her stare was disturbing.

"Did you think that he'd fallen asleep at the wheel?"

Alicia shrugged. John signaled to his best friend to cut the talk by making a slicing motion against his throat. He didn't want her to travel down the path of being responsible for the car accident.

"I don't get it. Why would Roy keep Dwayne's wrecked car? Do you think he was going to fix it up?" Brian asked. "That's the only reason I can think of. Or was he just sick with grief before—"

Both ideas turned his stomach. He could see how upset she was. A blank stare where he couldn't tell if she was aware he'd returned. He couldn't see inside the car, but it looked mangled.

"Did your father-in-law think he was responsible somehow? Is that why he killed himself?" Dev's question hung in the air.

John could only guess that Dev's research had turned up that information. He didn't know the answer. The man they'd known their entire lives would never have taken his own life. But none of the past mattered. People change after losing someone close to them. Only one person in the room could begin to understand what was in Roy's mind, but she remained silent. Not even a quick gasp of breath.

"We're missing something," Dev continued in his analytic mode. "Why wouldn't he get rid of the constant reminder of his son's accident?"

"Could he have thought there was a clue in the wreckage?" She looked hopeful and jumped to her feet, searching inside the car. "Could it still be here? Maybe you were right. Maybe that's why they killed him."

He quickly pulled her away to stop her. "If there had been, Roy would have turned it over to the cops."

"But—"

"I'm not following." Brian cut her off.

She turned to his brother, appearing ever hopeful for answers. "John thinks it's possible that Roy believed Dwayne was murdered. And then *he* was murdered to keep him from finding anything."

"Murdered? By who? Why?" Brian shouted.

No longer relaxed, his shoulders-back "fight me" stance called to John to respond in kind, but he held himself where he was. "I've got nothing but a gut feeling, that's all. Definitely not enough to base a plan on."

Brian hit the wall with his fist and the pacing began. "Son of a bitch, that's a giant place to leap for someone who hasn't been around for twelve years. Why are you doing this to her?"

"You weren't there tonight," Alicia said. "You didn't see Patrick and what he did. He killed Tory. Just shot her in cold blood right before the police pulled up. Yes, John's been gone. But maybe that's why he can consider what no one else has."

"You honestly think Roy Adams could commit suicide and leave Alicia here to fend for herself?" John asked his brother.

Brian drew a deep breath and turned into that mature son who helped their dad. "No one thinks it could happen to their family. I'm a paramedic. I see disbelief on people's faces all the time. Suicide, drugs, drunk driving. They all ask for proof. I'm sorry, Alicia. Guess I'm in the habit of not thinking much about it. I should have been there for you."

"You were," she answered softly, and returned to the chair.

"Did you say Weber shot someone named Tory?"

Dev asked. "Could her real name be Victoria, um, Strayhorn?"

"I think so." Alicia shrugged, leaned back and slipped out of her shoes. "She worked at Lauren's day care, and I can't remember her last name."

"Let me look at something." Dev walked to his gear just inside the double doors.

"Did you find the money?" John asked.

"What money?" Brian asked, following Dev and lifting electronic cases.

"No. But Patrick and Shauna are converting all their assets into cash," Dev said casually.

"We knew about the sale of property and horses." He didn't find anything strange in Shauna's getting rid of things that didn't interest her.

"I mean, *everything.* Stocks at a loss. Dissolving business partnerships for any amount of cash that can be forked over. *That* kind of cashing out."

"What money?" Brian asked again.

"Mind catching him up to speed, Dev, while I…?" He nodded to Alicia, who stared zombielike into the car again.

Followed by Brian, Dev went to the rental. He opened his laptop on the hood and began assembling whatever portable equipment he'd managed to bring from the cabin. If John knew the SEAL who prepared for everything—which he did—he knew the guy had the capability to hack the White House from his cell phone.

Brian asked questions. Dev answered. Alicia stared. Their conversation faded into the background. Should John get her out of here? Or make her face the demon rusting in the jumbled metal? He laid a hand on her shoulder and she jumped.

"Sorry. I… You see, no one really told me much when the accident happened. All the details were shared with Roy. It didn't matter to me since… I mean, he was dead, so it just didn't matter."

"I get it. Closure is different for everyone." He did understand. He'd written letters when he'd lost a man and then received answers from a couple of parents. One man wanted every detail he could divulge about the fight, while his wife had sent a letter to John's commander, asking why he'd commended her son's performance in battle. He got it, all right.

"I remember that he crashed and they couldn't get him out of the car. That's probably why there's no door. They probably had to pull it off, right? He died at the scene." Her voice was barely a whisper. "Roy handled everything."

"It's all right." He lowered his voice and knelt beside her. "This isn't a good place for you to be. If I'd known the car was here, I wouldn't have brought you."

"You can't protect me from the fact that my husband died, John. Accidents happen. Life happens." She squeezed his hand and he realized he'd been patting her knee. "In your line of work, you've probably seen your own share of tragedy."

He couldn't talk about what he'd seen. It wasn't fair to burden her with his nightmares. She had enough of her own. Dev's low voice wafted through the background as he explained to his brother what he'd been searching for in cyberspace.

"Something happened to you, John. I can see it. Every once in a while, you drift, and your sadness makes me want to snatch you back. You can tell me about it. I'm still here for you."

"Maybe someday." *Or never.* He stood, but she didn't release his hand. "We should get started, and you should get some more sleep."

"You need it more than me. How are you going to think of a great rescue plan while you're running on empty?" She crossed her legs and tugged off her socks.

"I'll catch twenty after Brian leaves."

"Then we should get started on the plan to get Lauren back before he has to head home," she said, stronger.

"You're right. We need a plan."

"How do you figure to accomplish a rescue?" Brian asked. "She'll be watched 24/7. No matter where they go."

"And if you do accomplish your goal, I haven't proved Alicia didn't plan everything," Dev added.

Their options were limited. They couldn't just

waltz up to the door and demand Alicia's daughter. Or could they?

"Exactly. That's why we're going to kidnap her during the auction today."

Chapter Twenty-Two

Once they'd worked most of the details out and the fine-tuning had come into play, Alicia had fallen into an emotional, exhausted sleep. She vaguely remembered John saying goodbye and maybe kissing her cheek.

With Brian's alibi established, the police couldn't connect him to Tory's shooting. So John planned to attend the auction using his brother's ID and be in position to orchestrate Lauren's kidnapping. Alicia had slept from dawn to about nine o'clock in the morning. Right until Dev had started his rental and driven off to purchase the rest of the gear they'd need.

A glance at her watch as she stretched awake for a second time told her it was nearly eleven. "I'm seriously hungry. Anything still in those saddlebags?"

"That's because you didn't eat before you fell asleep. Dev's almost back. Hope you like burgers for breakfast." Brian sat in the chair, looking so much like John it reminded her of when they'd all first met.

They were less gangly, had grown into handsome men and were good, helpful friends. As much as they tried to be different, they still had identical expressions and mannerisms.

"Anything will be much appreciated. Did he find the electronics he needed?"

"Yeah. That's a fairly big smile on your face, Miss Adams. Been a while since I've seen it where it belongs."

"You flirt. Am I smiling?" She laughed. "I'm happy this is almost over."

She was glad at the thought that Lauren would soon be back in her arms, protected, safe. The future after her rescue was still uncertain, but the most important thing was to get her daughter away from the murderers who had kidnapped her.

"Not all over. We still have to pull off a kidnapping and keep you guys out of sight until one of Dev's navy buds can track this money connection to Patrick. He passed it off to someone with a bigger computer."

"You don't sound too positive."

"Come on, Alicia. You think this chaotic plan of John's will work? Think he can act like a humble ranch hand again?" Brian pushed up from the chair, stretching and twisting as though he'd been stationary too long.

"To be honest, I can't *not* believe John and Dev know what they're doing. They rescue people in much more dangerous situations. Dev's not just some navy buddy, Brian. He's amazing with a computer."

Brian smiled once again. He might talk about her smiling, but he'd done more than his share since his fight with his brother. "And it hurt the guy to give in and call for help. Dev was in true pain. I guess you've had a bit more time to believe in John than I have. For twelve years I thought he was irresponsible—"

"And blamed him like the town blamed you."

"Uh," he began, and stopped himself. "Yeah, pretty much."

"Is that why you're so doom and gloom this morning?"

"I keep thinking of all the time I wasted." He rubbed his jaw. "The beatings I endured, the shunning of everyone except you and Mabel."

"Surely there's been a couple of others?"

"No one close. Hell, girl, I've never been on a serious date."

"You're kidding."

"I can't expose anyone to the treatment I live with just running to the grocery for a gallon of milk for Dad. And you know I can't move. I can't work more than three or four days in a row. Dad will work himself to death."

Alicia finger combed her hair and watched Brian shift uncomfortably on his feet. His confession must have been very difficult to make.

Instead of pacing around the barn like a caged lion, an action she'd seen often enough since his arrival, Brian stayed put. His eyes pleaded with her to understand. He was probably sharing thoughts he'd never told anyone. He was right. Who would he have explained to?

J.W. ate, worked, ate and went to bed. He had been a great friend to her father and Roy, but he wasn't from a generation of talkers. And unfortunately, Brian took after him more with every year that aged them all. John had been the one who always talked to her as they'd grown up. He, too, it seemed, had closed himself off. In two days, he hadn't said a word about his life over the past twelve years.

"I'm so sorry, Brian." She tried to imagine how lonely he'd been all these years. "But I think if you let someone fall in love with you, then they'd never doubt you were innocent."

"Is that why you've always believed in John?"

"What do you mean?"

"You believed that he didn't start the fire and wasn't there. You stood by him because you've always loved him." He stated it as matter-of-fact instead of really wanting to know the answer to a question. Just a little rise and fall of a firm shoulder. Acceptance that it was the way things had always been.

"I never believed you set the fire, either. Even after you confessed." She looked at him, wondering how the conversation had taken a turn to this place. "You know I love your whole family."

"Sweetheart, you do *not* love me and Dad like you do him." Brian laughed, completely at ease and relaxed. "And from the astonished look on your face, I think you're realizing that it's time to stop kidding yourself that you do."

"You're wrong. I don't. I can't. I loved Dwayne. I wouldn't have married him if I were still in love with Johnny. I'm just— Really, I can't possibly do that to Dwayne."

"Do what? Fall in love again?"

"Make people doubt our marriage. Or that I settled for him. Or that I was after his money. I couldn't." She dropped her head in her palms.

How could the world turn upside down in an instant yet again? She'd been so relieved that this ordeal would soon be over. So happy at the thought of seeing Lauren again and knowing she was safe. She'd actually been smiling, laughing. And now it was impossible.

No matter how much she cared about Johnny, she couldn't possibly be in love with him. It wasn't fair to Dwayne's memory. She felt a pat on her shoulder, then Brian's hand squeezed tight.

"No one will think you *settled* for either man. And there's not a single person in town who ever thought you married for money. I knew Dwayne. I was his best friend from the first peewee football team we were on. He'd be very happy for you both. I'm certain of that. You and Johnny are going to be good together."

One last squeeze and Brian walked outside, leaving her on her own.

Did she really love her high school sweetheart? Had she stopped only for the time she'd been with Dwayne? It might be true. Brian might be right about that, but he was certainly wrong about being good together.

John was a navy SEAL, for crying out loud. All he'd ever talked about in high school was joining the navy. He was a career man. He'd be leaving Aubrey and returning to his exciting world instead of living her day-to-day drama. After the dust settled from Shauna and Patrick's kidnapping, her world would be how to get a grape-jelly stain out of her favorite blouse. She'd patiently explained to him in the field that she'd never be with anyone again. So after all that straight talk, how could she change her story?

How could she possibly make him believe she loved him? And on top of all that…she hadn't known it until his brother had hit her over the head?

WEARING WESTERN BOOTS was a change that John welcomed. He would enjoy breaking in a new pair. If he had a reason to buy a pair again. Since Alicia had told him she'd never marry again—and he'd heard that underlying message of *especially him*—there wasn't much of a reason to think about moving back. He didn't have a reason to find a place to store boots in the barracks.

Brian hadn't been exaggerating about the number of people who avoided talking to him in town. There had been several women who were approaching and then had a sudden desire to stare into the hardware store window. The town truly had decided his brother's punishment.

And yet he was still here. Taking care of what was left of the ranch. Most definitely taking care of their dad. Always the responsible brother.

Brian had been right about the police officers, too. They weren't very good at tailing him. He gave them the slip long enough to meet Dev and receive the earbud and microphone. How and where his friend obtained his *toys* was beyond him. He was just grateful that he knew someone with that much talent.

He had to sit at the café lunch counter for a good ten minutes sipping coffee he didn't want or need before the cops showed up again. He needed them at the auction. Since Dev still hadn't located the money, if Patrick said or did anything, it was important to have reliable witnesses.

He was beginning to rethink the *reliable* about the time they pulled behind his granddad's truck to find him at the auction. Walking in a crowd of people who had shunned his brother brought back memories of the streets in Afghanistan. A foreigner in disguise on a rescue mission, praying no one knew his real identity.

Keep your cool, man. You'll get to tell these people off one day. Just not today.

"Everyone in place?" he asked just before he wouldn't be able to answer again without someone thinking it odd that he was talking to himself.

"Yes," Alicia answered hesitantly.

"Out of sight at the corral." Brian was in place for the distraction.

"Good to go, LT."

The line to register moved quickly and it was soon his turn. He filled out the information and returned the paper to the young woman. She smiled, clearly unaware of the treatment his brother normally received.

"What are you doing here, Sloane?" A man walked up to the registration desk. Dressed in a suit, obviously in charge. He knew Brian and each word showed his distaste at wasting his time on him.

"I thought it was an open auction." He couldn't wait to see this pompous ass eat his words.

"You're required to have a line of credit or cash to get inside. I already denied you that line of credit and I know no one else gave it to you. Unless you brought—"

John pulled the stack of bills from a bank envelope. "There's ten thousand. That enough to see if I want any of the Adamses' stock?"

"Where did you get that kind of money? You're broke."

"You don't really expect an answer, do you? Now, where's my bid number?" He put the cash away, looking around to see astonished faces everywhere. He could see the condemnation.

"I want this man thoroughly searched and if he has a weapon, hold him for the police."

John stepped to the side of the table and lifted his arms, forcing a smile to stretch from ear to ear, faking his ease at being frisked. He'd left his weapons behind for just this reason.

"They all believe I sell drugs," Brian said disgustedly, then laughed in his ear. "Now you just confirmed their suspicions and there will be worse rumors about why I haven't saved the ranch with the money before now."

"Don't distract him, man," Dev broke in. "Stay silent until you need to let us *all* know something."

Luckily Dev had intervened. John had been about to answer Brian himself. Go off on a rant right as he walked into the arena. His brother was the only person who could get a rise out him at this stage of an operation. He hadn't really been functioning at full SEAL capacity since he'd arrived in Texas.

Maybe he was losing his edge. Time to suck it up and focus. He knew he'd lost his heart for his chosen career months ago. He'd address his doubts after he secured Lauren. Walking from stall to stall of the animals for sale, he felt sick in his gut that Roy's life's work was about to disperse to parts unknown. These horses were Lauren's future. It was Alicia's decision to sell or keep them.

Avoiding a conversation with those around him wasn't hard. The locals kept their distance, and for the faces that tried to make eye contact, his angry expression should have put off a vibe that he wasn't too open for small talk. He didn't have to act interested in the stock—he genuinely was.

These were fine animals, good quarter-horse breeders his dad's ranch would be excited to own. He could hear the astonishment of the potential buyers as they chatted to each other. Some of the mares should never have gone to a public auction. They would go cheap because many of the bigger farms weren't represented. His fingers curled into fists. He had to grab the top rail of the corral to force his body to relax.

"Well, well, well. You never know what vermin will dare crawl out when there's food available."

"Hello, Shauna. It's been a while. Sorry to hear about everything your family's been going through."

"Right. Like I believe that." She parked herself in front of him, trapping him between a support beam and the stall of Roy's prize mare.

At least John had a view of the arena and could see Patrick chatting up the buyers.

"Making nice-nice with the enemy while I crawl through muck," Brian's voice was loud in John's ear.

"Come on, Brian. John's playing a part," Alicia said.

Just hearing her voice threw him out of step. "I'm, um, sorry, I didn't catch that."

"I said, we know your secret. We both know it's John who's helping Alicia." Shauna pretended to straighten his collar, lowering her voice so only he—and the rest of those on comm—could hear her. "I could have told the police, but Patrick convinced me to hold off. We don't know what you're trying to prove by attending the auction, but it's best if you turn around and leave."

John grabbed her wrists and pushed her away from him. Her little pout of hurt did nothing to him. He dealt with women acting like her in just about every bar he'd ever entered.

"If you believe that, Shauna, then call the cops over right now. I was eating pie at the diner last night when you claim I was in McKinney. The police have confirmed John is on a mission. He couldn't get home when Dad had his stroke and sure as hell doesn't care about any of our problems."

He made eye contact with Weber—still no sign of Lauren.

"Any possibility of me saying hello to Lauren today? You hiding her somewhere?"

"You're a horrible liar. Do you know that, John?" She tried to touch his head and he quickly pulled back. "Patrick and I think you're John."

"The auction's going to start soon and I've only seen half of the mares. I should be moving along." He tried to step around her. She moved into his path.

"Now, we both know you're really here to try to get our little angel." She laid on the Southern twang and put a finger over her heart while she glanced upward. "You can try to take her from us, but as you can see, she's being guarded very well today."

Shauna pointed to the security guards and then to…

Gargantuan.

He stood in the general direction Weber had been a few minutes before. Lauren was evidently holding his hand, but he couldn't see her through the crowd. The giant towered over everyone and it was easy to keep him in his peripheral vision. He seemed to be headed, along with most of the other attendees, to the midsection of risers in front of the center arena.

"You won't take her from me. I promise you that."

"Were you saying something, Shauna? Dang, I didn't hear a word of it. Guess I got lost thinking how well that mare will look with my stock. Pardon me." He'd heard every senseless word. With all the huffing and puffing she was doing, it was fairly obvious that not caring what she had to say sent her into a tizzy.

He looked over her shoulder, past most of the crowd and saw Patrick's hand slap the wall. *He* was the one listening. That was why Shauna was all over him. They were hoping he'd give something away.

Again he tried to move around her, but she grabbed his arm.

"You can pretend not to care all you want, but that guard doesn't earn a penny if Lauren leaves his side. I believe you've already discovered just how good of a fighter he is." She touched the side of his jaw where a darkening bruise had formed.

"That? I got whacked by a tree branch, tracking down a coyote that's been stalking my stock. One thing you should know—I protect what's mine." He placed his hands on her shoulders, keeping her in one spot as he passed.

Three voices burst loudly into his ear. He was

afraid he winced in pain or, worse yet, it had been so loud that others near him would have heard. Everyone went about their business as usual. Shauna stomped back to Weber at the entrance, pushing people out of the way, then smiling sweetly as she said thank-you.

Whatever Alicia and Dev said was lost under Brian's distinctive, "What the heck was that all about?"

"She's wired," Dev suggested after they quieted. "Gotta be. No way they'd keep the info that you were here to themselves."

"Would have been easy for the cops to find out. My prints are on file and if you left any at that shindig last night—"

"Not a chance."

"Then they're either shooting in the dark or working with the cops," Brian surmised. "Why the hell would she be playing footsie in the corner with you?"

"Can you see Lauren?"

"She's sitting next to the bodyguard. Same guy as at the house." He barely moved his lips to give his team the info.

"You need help?" Brian laughed. "Do we stick with the plan? Or call it quits?"

"We never quit, just adapt," Dev answered before John could.

"Affirmative. A diversion about now would be great."

John took the steps two at a time to the top of the risers. Gargantuan continued to look in Weber's direction, but behind him. The only part about this extraction he didn't like was that Lauren and her mom would be watching him succeed or fail.

He would *not* fail.

Chapter Twenty-Three

"Distraction number one, on its way."

John listened for signs that his brother might be in trouble. The sound of metal connecting with metal would be the vent cover being screwed back into place. The smoke bomb that Brian lit would be safe and nontoxic to breathe. It would irritate eyes more than anything else.

It didn't take long for someone to point to the gray smoke trickling, then pouring, from the air vents. The homemade smoke bomb should burn long enough to fill the arena. Long enough for authorities to be called.

If they accomplished nothing else, at least Roy's stock wouldn't be sold off today.

No one yelled *fire*. No one created panic. Several auction workers quietly moved through the crowd and gestured toward the exits. John took out his cell and attempted to search for an internet connection. If anyone asked why he was sitting in a smoke-filled room, he'd use it as an excuse to be unaware of his surroundings. Several people had already looked up in surprise after their heads had been bowed, praying to their smartphones.

Everyone exited quickly. It had gone as efficiently as they'd hoped. Alicia had asked all three of them to promise no one would get hurt. She was riddled with guilt over Tory's death. It didn't matter how many times they'd all assured her that Weber had been intent on killing the witnesses.

An option thrown around in their early-morning planning had been to just snatch Lauren and run with her. But it had been shot down, since the police would be all over them before they got to the main road. No, they had to create a situation where the Webers were separated from her. And to get that to happen, Gargantuan needed to take her outside.

A smoke-filled room and he didn't budge.

Workers argued with the giant, and Lauren sat unnaturally quietly at his side.

Had they drugged her? Threatened her? If the bastards had hurt Alicia's little girl, he wouldn't be able to restrain himself. *I swear I'll use every skill I've ever been taught as a SEAL. No holds barred.*

Lauren coughed and covered her face. *Leave. Get her out of here before I have to take matters into my own hands.*

"Sir, you really must go outside."

"What? Sorry, slow Wi-Fi." John was focused

on Gargantuan and hadn't noticed the young man at his side. "Hey, is there a fire?" He searched for signs of Weber. Neither Patrick or Shauna were in sight. "Do you know where the people in charge are relocating?"

He didn't give a hill of beans where anyone running the auction was located. He wanted Weber in his sights. He'd never thought Weber would leave Lauren with someone else, but that scenario most definitely worked in their favor.

"I just know that we need to get out of here." The man sternly laid a hand on his shoulder, encouraging John to leave. Since the giant was leaving, too, John was ready.

"Lead the way. Don't let me slow you down."

"Assuming that was a disguised question for me," Dev said in his earpiece, "Mrs. Witch is in the car waiting with the engine running—probably cooling down. I still can't believe how freakin' hot it is here in Texas. My bad, no eyes on Weber."

"If they're acting like the concerned grandparents, then why did they both leave Lauren alone with that man?" Alicia asked. "And I agree with Dev that it's dang hot out here with all these layers of clothes on."

"Are you in place, Nurse Adams?"

"Yes, I am."

"Did you say something?" the guy escorting him outside asked.

"Just thanks, man." John ducked back to the registration area to watch for Gargantuan's exit. He'd heard the big man give in after the threat of calling security. And seconds later, he appeared, carrying Lauren on his hip.

"Ladies and gentlemen, there wasn't a fire." Someone shouted the announcement.

"She looks so scared," Alicia whispered.

Strange how he could hear her slightest whisper and pick her out instantly in the crowd. He assumed the rest of the announcement that he missed actually stated they'd begin the auction again soon, since people turned around and began talking instead of continuing to their cars.

"She stopped sucking her fingers months ago."

The giant headed to the car on the far side of the offices. John caught a glimpse of Lauren, fingers in her mouth, sad eyes watering not only from the smoke but also from constant tears.

"Focus on your job, Alicia. Don't look at anything else. Only your job, hon. That's it." John spoke into the cell phone so he wouldn't appear to be a crazy man just talking to himself. He should have obtained a wireless headset so his hands would be completely free.

He watched the woman he would give up everything for waddle toward him. A blond wig completely changed the way she looked. The padding making her look two hundred pounds helped a lot, too. Man, she must be boiling in all those extra clothes.

The police and fire truck arrived right on cue. Sirens blasted into the chaos and ceased just as fast. The men poured from their vehicles, quickly trying to assess what was wrong. The horses in the paddock nickered, getting more agitated as more smoke blew in their direction and the crowd got louder.

"You're almost up, Dev. Gargantuan's on his phone. He's headed to the car with Lauren." He stashed the cell in his pocket as Alicia pretended to trip and fall to the ground.

"Do you need some assistance, ma'am?" He was right there to help her. While he pulled her upright, she slipped his weapon inside his belt and covered it with his shirt. "Just remember, if everything goes off without a hitch, we'll have Lauren back before they know she's gone."

As hot as it was, he missed her when she'd stepped away from his hold.

"I certainly hope you're right."

"Piece of cake."

"I can't believe you said that, John," Dev whined.

"Why? What does Dev mean?" she asked, looking up at John with the same sad, worried eyes of her daughter. The tension and stress of the past few days had begun to show in the dark circles, but she was still the most beautiful woman around. Especially to him.

He had completely fallen for Alicia Adams—nurse, mother, friend. He could freely admit that he had it bad. But who would he tell? His best friend, who would try to talk him out of leaving the navy? His brother? Things were better, but he didn't feel like discussing a future with Alicia with him. Not yet.

"He just jinxed us. I'd elaborate, Alicia, but a cop is walking right toward me. Going off comm. Excuse me, Officer?"

"Dev's a superstitious old woman, that's all. He thinks it brings us bad luck to say an operation will be easy." He smiled, trying to reassure her. He didn't know if it worked. They had to separate before they drew more attention to themselves.

He also didn't want her to ask if Dev's superstitions were founded in truth. Unfortunately, they were. He hadn't been the person to say it back then, but he remembered how things had gone south real fast on ops that should have been easy ins and outs.

John stayed in the center of everything. Making eye contact with as many people as possible. Staying visible. Making certain Brian could not be accused of any part of this. If things went bad it would be on *his* head. Not Brian's.

He caught the silent version of his buddy's performance. It appeared convincing enough—at least from a hundred yards away.

Dev showed the Aubrey officer fake county Child Protection Services credentials and pointed to where Gargantuan had set Lauren on the back of Shauna's car. Where the man had obtained the necessities—earbuds, costumes, fake credentials— to pull this stunt off in such a short time, he had no idea. It definitely made him appreciate that his friend had come to watch his back and lend a hand. Or two. Or three.

The officer split the crowd, and Dev, dressed like a bent-over old man, followed. The officer showed the paper to Gargantuan, who immediately banged on the rear window of the car.

"Why are you still here?"

John spun in the direction his shoulder was being yanked. "Weber."

"You're behind all this smoke business, and when I find out how, you'll be in jail for good this time."

"Yes, it has been a long while, Patrick. Glad things are going so well for you."

"Why, I should—"

"Hit me? Go for it. Take your best shot, man." John wanted to throw the first punch. Wanted to make this piece of worthless scum bleed and beg for him to stop.

"Hey, John, hang on there, bro."

Brian interrupted his mental picture of tearing Weber to shreds. It would have been nice.

"Stick to the plan, Johnny," Alicia said. "Forget him. We need Lauren."

Today the objective was the rescue of an innocent four-year-old girl. One day it would be the arrest of the murderer in front of him. He hoped it would be his testimony that locked this rat away and sent him to death row in the Huntsville State Prison.

The *rat's* cell phone was buzzing like crazy. If he could keep Weber occupied for five more minutes, Dev might have everything wrapped up and be able to get to safety without any trouble at all. Let Shauna handle CPS taking Lauren into protective custody. Weber's involvement might slow Dev down. The more his friend was questioned, the more opportunity there was to mess up.

"What do you want from me, Weber? I just came to buy some horses."

Weber shoved at his shoulder. "I want you to leave. I've told everyone that your drug money's no good here. You'll never get your hands on Adams's stock. Your family's always been a second-rate quarter-horse farm and that's what you'll continue to be."

Weber removed his shades. His dead eyes stared while one side of his mouth tilted into a smirk. "Or have you been gone too long to notice, John?"

Damn, his fingers itched to curl into a fist and

lay this guy flat, teaching him a lesson or two along the way. Especially the lesson of the Sloane brothers. It didn't matter which one you were dealing with.

"Don't do it, John. They'll throw me in jail before you can blink. Remember, you're me right now."

"I got that," John answered his brother. Fortunately, the answer worked for Weber, too. If Weber drew him into a fight or acknowledging his identity, it would be more difficult to complete their mission.

"Then get out." Weber's cell buzzed again and he reached into his pocket.

Don't let him look at it. "There's one thing I don't get at all."

His opponent—even if only sparring with words—rolled his shoulders and angled his stance, ready to throw a punch. "I can't wait to hear. As if your opinion means anything to anyone around here."

Yeah, Weber was razzing up the crowd, upsetting them, reminding them of the past and another fire. John could hear their murmuring. He hated that Brian had fought this battle for so long on his own.

"I don't get how things work at your ranch, Weber. Remind me. With no horses or stock, we might have to call it something else, and there really isn't any word. But that doesn't matter. Who's in charge? Do you take orders from Shauna or her money? How does it feel selling off the horses you actually worked with in the stables?"

"Why, you…"

John prepared for the punch. He was going to roll on the ground right into the legs of the crowd gathering at their raised voices.

"Mr. Weber, there's an emergency at your car. They've been trying to get you on your phone." Weber's fist was raised and ready to strike, but he dropped it as soon as the messenger spoke his name.

"Dev has Lauren. The officer's escorting him to his car," Alicia said.

"See, piece of cake. No extra work involved," Brian quoted the mantra of the day.

"I may not be able to have you arrested, but I can do one thing." Weber dusted his hands off and gestured to one of his workers nearby. "Escort him off the property and see that he doesn't return."

John shrugged out of the hands of the man attempting to "escort" him to his truck. They needed Dev to have Lauren out of sight when Weber realized he'd lost her. John was certain he'd blow his top, and he wanted witnesses. But the unknown factor was that they didn't know if Weber had friends in the Aubrey police who might detain a CPS administrator until confirmation could be obtained from county.

So Dev had to be out of sight. He was only to his car, buckling Lauren into the child-safety seat.

"Tell me when they're out of here and completely clear."

"Huh?" the guy shoving him to the parking lot said.

Both Brian and Alicia confirmed and kept feeding him the details.

Another push between his shoulder blades and John had had enough. "Come on, man. I can walk faster if I'm not tripping every time you push. I'm leaving, so back off."

Most of the crowd had migrated toward the so-called emergency with Weber. The guy shoved again.

"Am I in the clear?" John asked.

"That's an affirmative," his brother answered, imitating Dev's voice. "Everyone's watching the show Shauna's putting on."

"Buddy, you ain't never going to be in the clear in Aubrey." The man—John thought he was the younger brother of someone they'd gone to school with—shoved again.

John didn't trip. Or budge.

But he did turn around.

Chapter Twenty-Four

Donny Ashcroft marched John to the parking lot just like Patrick had instructed. He hit John again in the middle of his back, but this time John didn't move. He pivoted and fired off a right cross that dropped Donny to the ground like a fly. Alicia watched from the corner of the building and tried not to giggle. Poor man, his jaw would really hurt for a while. It wasn't nice to hit someone when they weren't looking. But in all fairness, John had asked the guy to stop pushing.

"Dev's driving through the gate," Brian stated.

She waved to John so he'd know where to find her, but he followed after Patrick. There was a determined look on his face. The same one that had been there when he'd taken her away from Lauren last night.

"Let's get out of here." Brian's uneasiness was plain in his shaky voice.

"He needs to be down the street and around the corner. We can't risk anyone catching a glimpse of the license tags on the rental." John ran into the crowd.

"I've got another smoke grenade."

"Use it. We need the cops occupied here. Not pursuing Dev."

"But, John, Brian's in the paddock with the horses and they're already skittish." *Apprehensive* didn't begin to describe the level of nervousness thrumming throughout her body. For a couple of minutes there, it was almost over—right up to the word *pursuing.* When would everything be back to normal?

But did she want the return of her *normal?*

"Do it," John commanded, and ran in the direction Patrick had gone. "We don't have a choice."

Seconds later smoke billowed toward the sky on the far side of the corral. The horses neighed excitedly. They smelled the smoke and didn't know there wasn't a fire. She knew how they felt, scared to death by the unknown.

The makeshift fat suit she wore was cumbersome and stifling in this heat. And the wig was horrid and itchy. It was like having straw stuck into a woolen cap. They'd thrown her layer of fat together by stuffing clothing from the secondhand store into an outdated pantsuit. She couldn't wait to be out of this costume and back with Lauren. Before that could happen, they had to give Dev time to get away.

But she couldn't do anything except stand to the side and watch.

John's look after he'd punched Donny brought back more memories than of losing Lauren or Tory's death. Now she'd visually lost track of both brothers and was afraid of what John might do. She could hear noise and thought she caught bits of words through her ear microphone thingy, but they weren't clear enough to distinguish.

Dev was at his car, and the police officer had joined the firemen returning from the corral. She joined the back of the crowd and resorted to good old-fashioned face-to-face communication to find out what was happening.

"What's going on now?" She didn't ask anyone specifically and received a slew of answers.

"There's a fight."

"It's Sloane and that big man."

"Isn't that the Weber bodyguard?"

"I heard the police took Lauren Adams away."

"That must have crushed Shauna."

Once the people started gossiping, they wouldn't shut up. Some of them believed the media propaganda. Others didn't believe a word of what they saw on television. They all crowded together and wanted to see the fight between John and the man he referred to as Gargantuan.

A collective *oh* rang through the crowd as they

witnessed a punch. All she saw were two arms soaring backward through the air.

Under her breath she added, "That looked like John flying backward." And then louder she asked, "Who's winning?" She was still unable to see over the heads in front of her. She had to get out of here before she passed out from heat and a lack of clear air.

"I can't say for sure, but I think John may be getting his butt kicked by this guy." Brian's voice shot inside her head like a DJ on the radio. It was a strange feeling, having someone chat in your ear. But also a comforting feeling, having them right beside you. She wanted to turn and glare at his words. In spite of their content, his friendly voice—so like John's—was comforting to hear and meant he was still close enough to help.

"What was he thinking?"

"I don't believe it was his idea. But it's just the distraction we needed while the fire department clears away my smoke. He'll be okay, Alicia. Don't worry."

"Is Dev gone?"

"Can't see any sign of the car, and the smoke seems to have gotten the police interested in real business instead of being ordered around by Patrick," Brian said.

"The police may want to get a handle on the crowd's rowdiness and not stand around watching the fight." Alicia pushed her way through to the corral fence where several men had climbed for a better view. The horses were crowding each other, and if one of these men fell under them— Well, she knew who would be blamed for their injuries.

"We have to stop this before someone gets hurt."

"Not so sure we can do that. John told me to get you out of here."

"Well, come and get me," she taunted, knowing he couldn't come to her. They'd all go to jail if he did. But even if he could, Brian would have to drag her, kicking and screaming. She couldn't run away and leave John. He'd never do that if she were in danger.

"It appears that two teams have formed—those for John and those against. If we're not careful, there's going to be a full-blown riot here." No one could hear her talking to herself over the crowd noise. Or no one seemed to pay attention.

"Is it nice to know that so many people care about you and Lauren?" Brian asked.

"I hear them talking about you, too."

"Humph." She could see that Sloane brow rising, questioning if it actually mattered at this point or not. It did; they just didn't have time to talk about it.

"How do we stop this fight?"

The auction had drawn ranchers from several cities, but there were still lots of Aubrey citizens around, egging on the beating of Brian Sloane.

They wouldn't have cared if it had been John. Those people believed both brothers were guilty of the death of a beloved teacher. When several opened the corral and shoved the fight into the middle of the already panicked horses, she knew it wasn't going to end well.

If Gargantuan didn't kill John, the horses would. And two-thirds of those in this crowd would let it happen.

"We can't show our faces, Alicia. Think of Lauren's safety."

"But—"

"Stick to the plan. Your turn to leave."

Stick to the plan. It was exactly like John issuing an order. "And then what?"

"Huh?" Brian wasn't the only one paying attention. Those closest to her had given her an extra look or two to see if she was talking to them.

"And then what? We wait on him to be thrown in jail or worse?" She tapped the leg of the man sitting nearest her on the fence and recognized him. Dusty Phillips had bought several horses from Roy before. "Mr. Phillips, can't you please do something to stop this?"

"Why would I want to?" he said before glancing down at her. "Is that you, Alicia? I thought you… What in the world are you wearing?"

The men had rolled and become more visible. The crowd was chanting and she could see that

Gargantuan had his forearm across John's larynx, choking him.

"Never mind me, can't you help him? If he passes out, the horses will trample him."

"Get out of there," Brian yelled in her ear. "That guy knows you. John will do a lot worse to me if you're caught."

Dusty shook his head and gripped the white steel rail tighter. "The cops are right there, why not ask them?"

"You know they won't help. Won't somebody stop this?"

"I will, Alicia," Dusty's wife said. "Anyone who's met you and seen you with your little girl knows there's no way you'd do what they're accusing you of. Good luck getting things straightened out. Come on, Dusty."

The couple threw their legs over the fence and dropped in with the horses. Alicia wasn't worried for them. Both Dusty and Carla had been around horses since birth. Carla was a champion barrel racer, and Dusty faced down bulls on a regular basis. Going through the pen was definitely quicker than through the crowd.

Alicia had no idea what Carla intended to do. John was a trained SEAL and hadn't managed to break free.

"Time for this to end, guys," Carla yelled at the police, then looked up at the onlookers. "Craig,

David, Kerry, come on, this isn't right. You going to let him choke to death?"

The three men jumped down to the soft dirt and joined Dusty. It took all four of them to pull at the giant to get him to budge.

"Are you really going to just stand there?" Carla shamed the police officer and security guard into helping. Men hopped off the gate and opened it for the two men.

"Remember this, Brian. They think it's you out there."

John had been right. Gargantuan was unbelievably strong, but he was also very intent on not giving up. John twisted, kicked and finally gasped for air.

Alicia's insides seemed to bounce off her skin. Panic? She didn't seem to have any air, either.

The men pulled and pried at the thick hand clasped in place. Then John was free, gulping air. And she could breathe again with him. She was light-headed from just holding her breath. What did John feel like? But he didn't stop. He was on his feet, fists raised, waiting for a second round.

"Come on, Alicia. The cops can take care of the rest. We need to get out of here."

"I'm sort of stuck here."

Everyone wanted to see what was happening and kept pressing her closer and closer to the fencing. Four men could barely hold the giant who'd nearly killed John. She thought the police officer was trying to arrest the huge man.

As John backed up into the unsettled horses, he looked at her, pointed to his ear and shook his head. "I don't think John can hear us anymore."

"Do I need to come get you?" Brian asked.

Initially, she hadn't thought that a hundred people in an open area could trample a person. But confined as she was in her "fat suit," she was beginning to feel trapped. If she could take it off and squeeze through the fence rails, she could hide behind the horses and join John inside the building.

"Go. I'm okay, Brian. I'll meet you there."

Thank goodness she'd kept yoga pants and a tank on under the makeshift baggy clothes they'd filled with padding. Undressing took longer than she wanted, pressed where she was, but she managed. Even the hot metal of the railing touching her skin was cooler than being wrapped inside all those clothes had been. She could probably get out the way she'd come, but it would put her at greater risk than slipping in with the horses. The Phillipses had made such a quick trek through them.

Piece of cake, as Johnny said.

The lovely stock the Adamses had spent so many decades developing circled the paddock, still nervous, but calming as the smoke completely cleared.

Now was the perfect time. With all eyes on Gargantuan's removal to the police car, she slipped through the fence rails, pulled all her clothing through and bundled it in her arms. Then she was off. She bent as far as she could, trying not to be seen above the horses' backs.

She was close. She could see the door leading to the individual stalls. She'd almost made it when the horses stopped circling and all loped away toward the gate. Loud shouting she couldn't understand could be heard over the horses' frightened neighing and angry snorts. She was rooted to the ground, not knowing which way the horses would move next.

Gunshots. Two, then three pops.

The whinnying grew. The horses wanted away from the danger and would stampede any second. The mare next to her reared. Alicia froze, staring at its underbelly and lashing forelegs.

Chapter Twenty-Five

John's voice was stuck somewhere other than his throat. Maybe Gargantuan had broken the cords, because they wouldn't work. No warning. No question. No nothing. Watching Alicia drop to the ground was the first time he'd ever frozen in fear.

He'd been in firefights in the middle of the Afghanistan desert and not been this frightened. Had the horse kicked her? Was she unconscious? Her arms covered her head while curled in a ball on the ground. She was covered with colorful sweaters and T-shirts and pajama bottoms. It didn't look real, and if he hadn't been paralyzed from the fright coursing through his veins, he might have wondered if it was a dream.

No, this was real. Dev and his dang jinx. Alicia hadn't moved. If he yelled to see if she was conscious, the horses would just spook again. It would have been easier if he hadn't lost the earbud in the fight.

A quick assessment of his surroundings showed

the corral gate closed. Gargantuan was now secured inside the cop's car. They were hauling Shauna away for some reason and she was fighting them tooth and nail, screaming obscenities about Weber. Lauren was safe—Dev had texted. He'd heard gunshots. No signs of anyone down or in pursuit.

The mare still pawed at the ground. Folks on the other side of the rail began pointing to the pile of clothes. Then he saw her fingers wiggle. So did the horse.

"Don't move, sweetheart. I'm coming to you. Just stay calm."

The horses continued to dance around. Some guys on the other side of the paddock were trying their best to settle the herd. But they couldn't get to Alicia. He was her only chance.

His girl would move a little, but the colored clothing would move a lot. Then the horse would spook again. "Still, sweetie," he sung to both Alicia and the mare. "Just sit tight...almost there."

All the horses wore halters so they could be led easily in the arena. He just needed to grab... The mare reared her head and twisted out of his reach. "I'm close, hear me, hon? You okay?"

"Yes," she whispered.

"I'm reaching for her halter. Now, when I get it, you know she may buck, so be prepared. Can you see her hooves?"

"I'm ready."

"Great. One more step. And…got it."

The mare danced, hooves prancing in all directions, but he was able to back her hindquarters to the rail and contain most of the pawing away from Alicia. "You're clear. Stand up and let's get out of here. Lauren's safe. Time for her mom to be the same."

She sat, a bright yellow sweater fell to the dark dirt and applause burst out. John finally noticed everyone watching him. And he noticed the two horse wranglers who were calming and removing the horses back to their stalls. One came and took the frightened mare.

John stretched out his arms and pulled Alicia straight to connect her lips to his. A kiss that soothed his soul and hopefully hers. He didn't care if she was ready or not. He wouldn't lose her. She needed to know she was his.

"Don't ever scare me like that again." He wanted to shake her until she swore, but instead he kissed her some more. And she definitely kissed him back.

There was more applause.

"Wow."

"I agree. Maybe the crowd thinks I'm Brian, but I don't care. Dev sent a message as soon as he arrived at the location with Lauren. Hey, you're not putting any weight on your left foot."

"No, the mare stepped—"

He swung her into his arms, leaving the sweaters and pajama pants in the dirt. Her arms were locked tightly around his neck as he strode inside. "Can you tell me what possessed you to stroll into a herd of half-spooked horses?"

His lips couldn't resist touching her forehead, where a soft tendril of hair had escaped its bobby pin.

"I didn't stroll anywhere. I was trying to get out of that crowd and follow you."

"You're lucky they only stepped on your ankle and not your skull."

He continued to the side door of the stables, intent on getting them as far away as possible. Everyone at the auction knew Alicia had been there. And it wouldn't be too long before they confirmed that Lauren hadn't been taken by CPS.

"I think you can put me down now." She adjusted her head and cheek closer to the curve of his shoulder, giving every indication she was comfy resting in his arms.

Tired, physically exhausted, he was more than happy to hold her next to him. He ached to put her down and kiss her into oblivion and back again.

"Let's go. After all we've been through, I don't want you or *Brian* to be arrested. Or wait in a jail cell while the police sort everything out. After they connect his prints to the kidnapping house, Gargantuan will sing for a reduced sentence, connecting Weber to Tory's murder. Then Weber will—"

"Weber will what?" the man in question asked, stopping John in his tracks. He leaned against the side of the stables, an unconscious auction worker at his feet, a 9 mm Glock pointed straight at them. "Weber might just blow your brains out in self-defense right now. Or he could wait. Do you know which he'll choose, John?"

Weber was a killer who didn't fit a profile. You couldn't predict what he would do or when. He could pull the trigger without warning in the blink of an eye. It was the one type of profile that scared John more than those horses trying to stampede in the corral.

"What do you want, Patrick?" Alicia asked, tightening her grip around John's neck.

"Me? I don't want a thing. I'm here capturing the fugitives who've somehow fooled authorities, kidnapped my four-year-old step-granddaughter and caused my wife to shoot at the bodyguard."

"That's why they put her in handcuffs." Alicia had a little wonder in her voice. "She fired the shots and then was arrested. Oh, my, how awful."

John could tell she tried not to smile, but she was happy Shauna was in custody.

Weber rolled his eyes and casually waved his gun. "I can see you're all broken up. No escape for you this time. Having a getaway car hidden somewhere like last night won't help you today."

"My car is in the lot next to the rest, keys are

under the mat. That is, if you need a getaway car. I'm sure you're worried about your giant cohort talking to the police." Alicia dropped her arm, sliding it down his back.

Switching her gaze to John, she mouthed, *Let me down.* As he set her feet gently below her, her hand tugged at the tail of his shirt, slipped under it and lifted the SIG she'd brought to him earlier.

"Do you really think no one's going to catch you, Patrick?" she asked when she faced Weber, keeping the gun pressed against John's back. "There are an awful lot of people who know the truth now. You can't shut all of them up."

How were they going to get the SIG into his hand to defend them?

"You're such a bore, Alicia. Drop the gun that you're obviously trying to get and be done with it."

Alicia let the SIG hit the ground before John could deny it was there, bouncing between his feet.

"Kick it and let's get moving."

He kicked the gun about two feet in front of himself. Only two feet. He could dive and get off several rounds, but not before the psycho pointing his weapon at Alicia would squeeze the trigger.

"Where are we going?" she asked.

"Talking is such a tiresome strategy. It won't stop me from killing you."

"I should hope not."

"What?" John asked together with a surprised Weber.

"Well, um, it would indicate that we're stupid, for one thing. And I don't think any of us are stupid." She faced John and mouthed, *Play along,* then pointed to her ear. "Bullheaded and stubborn, maybe. But not stupid."

He didn't understand her sudden desire to communicate with Weber.

"You know what, Patrick? I'm pretty tired and hot. I'm going to sit right here on this tack box until you make up your mind where we're supposed to go. Aren't you tired, Brian?" She nodded her head and patted the wood next to her so dramatically John knew she was up to something. She tugged him with her, keeping the gun on the ground just out of his reach.

Then he got it. Her microphone and receiver were still working. Brian must be in the wings giving her instructions.

"Get up. Hands where I can see them, John. It is John. Don't bother to deny it."

"Who's denying?" He shrugged and stayed put. "It feels good to sit and rest a minute. It's so dang hot out here and my feet hurt. They aren't used to the boots."

"Get up. Both of you. Now!"

"I don't think so, Patrick." Alicia stared at Weber but tapped John's leg, then pulled up on her black, stretchy tights. She pointed toward the ground. Stuck securely inside her socks, next to her ankle-bone, was a sweet snub-nosed pistol. She massaged her legs, coming up the last time palming the gun to where Patrick couldn't see it.

"I love you," he announced, not caring who heard—or threatened their lives. She smiled, looking confident that he'd handle the problem.

He slid his hand over hers and took the gun, pointing it at Weber as he spoke. "We'll wait right here for the cops. Or you pull the trigger and run from the cops, who are most likely on their way already. You go ahead and run in this heat. I'm with my gal here, we're sitting."

Weber looked stunned, totally thrown off while he tried to determine what game they were playing. Then something darkened in his eyes. The confusion cleared and the sinister soul from last night looked at him.

"Stubborn fools."

"Actually, Patrick, I told you we weren't stupid. Why would we ever make killing us easy for you?"

John saw the moment of decision. A microsecond where he knew Weber was tired of the game and would pull the trigger. He raised the snub-nose, pushed Alicia backward off the tack box and fell sideways on top of her.

As he fell, he heard Weber's gun fire and saw the kickback in his forearm. Slow motion had nothing on waiting to find out where the bullet would hit. Low. Wood splintered. Weber stepped toward the stables for another shot at them both. John fired when he stepped into his sights.

The bullet caught Weber in the shoulder. His weapon fell to the ground as he dropped to his knees. But Weber didn't stop. He reached for the gun, raising it toward his head.

John pictured sitting on the stand, testifying, putting this deranged man behind bars and letting justice decide his punishment. "You're not getting off—" John fired "—that easy."

The weapon dropped to the ground a second time. A twice-shot, but very much alive, Weber fell the opposite direction.

"Is it over?" Alicia asked from under him.

"Sorry, honey." He crawled off her and returned to the tack box, helping her join him.

Brian ran around the corner, breathing hard.

"Where have you been?" John asked his brother.

Sheriff Coleman trotted behind him, didn't stop at the corner and kept trotting his large frame to Weber. He clicked the microphone on his shoulder. "He's alive. Where's that ambulance?"

"He'd better be alive. My team would have my marksmanship ribbon if I'd killed him without trying."

"He killed Tory Strayhorn and orchestrated Lauren's kidnapping," Alicia said. "He may have killed

Roy. Shauna's just as guilty and wanted to kill us. She knew what was going on, Ralph. Everything. And—" she turned back to Brian, finally drawing a breath "—where's Lauren? When can I see her?"

"Whoa, slow down, Alicia. It's okay," Brian assured her. "Dev's on his way to the ranch. He'll be there before us."

"Thank goodness. But the police don't know what they did. Who do we need to explain things to? Can I see Lauren before they ask for our statements?"

"I have a feeling the police already know. Otherwise they'd be arresting us." Lauren was safe and John wanted Alicia alone. Now. Before they were required to give statements or explain why they'd avoided the police.

"Shauna and Gargantuan are claiming their innocence. Shouting that it was all Weber's idea from the start. Including Roy's supposed suicide." Brian gave him a sign that they should escape while they could. "Maybe you two should cut out before they realize they need to talk to you. I think there's a little girl at home that's missing her mommy."

"Yes, please? Will it be okay to leave?"

"I'll tell Ralph to come by after dinner. Looks like they have their hands full right now anyway." Brian stuck out his hand to bring John to his feet, pulling him into a quick bear hug.

It was a step toward reconciliation that John

needed. But there was something else he had to find out first.

He swung Alicia into his arms again, remembering she couldn't walk. He preferred that she didn't walk, liking her just where she was. "Do you need a medic to look at your ankle?"

"It's just bruised and will be sore. I can walk."

"Not a chance. Still got that earbud?"

"Yes. It took you long enough to realize. Brian kept telling me to stall and then he'd shout at people or tell me not to be an idiot and tick Patrick off."

"Do me a favor."

"Anything." She snuggled closer and kissed his voice box with whisper-soft kisses.

"Hand the earpiece to Brian. Dev's going to have my hide for losing one. I have no idea what he'd do if I lost two."

"But I haven't lost mine."

Brian walked forward and took it from her anyway.

"No tellin' where it's going to end up in just a little while."

"Where are you taking me?" she asked sweetly, holding tighter to his neck.

"Does it matter?"

She smiled as an answer. She didn't make an excuse or try to convince him to stay for the sheriff or police. There was a car in the parking lot. He'd told her he loved her; now it was time to find out if that was enough.

"You may be ready...or not, Alicia. But here I come."

Chapter Twenty-Six

"Why, Johnny Sloane, are you trying to get me into the backseat of your car? Bringing me out to the middle of nowhere didn't even work in high school. I'm flattered, but I'd really like to see my little girl."

Alicia joked, but she had no idea where they were going. The air-conditioning felt wonderful on full blast, so they weren't melting in the heat.

"I only need a couple of minutes alone with you. Just a couple. Promise," he said, nibbling at her fingertips laced through his strong hand. "I don't think either of us will fit back there as comfortably as we did when we were teenagers."

He turned toward the ranch, but he'd given her the impression they weren't headed straight home. Maybe he'd changed his mind and was taking her to Lauren after all.

"I am ready. I was wrong last night, or this morning, whatever time it was out in the field."

He kissed the back of her hand. "I know."

"Where are we going?"

"There's something I need to do here."

"But this is…" *The fire.*

"Yeah, it's Mrs. Cook's place."

"Why do you need to come to where the fire happened?"

"Closure. Coming full circle. It just seems appropriate."

He stopped in the field where they'd parked as teens. The old barn had burned to the ground back then. Any remnants had been cleared away. But there was a familiar tree and stone wall that he led her to.

The last place they'd argued. He offered to pick her up, but she wanted to walk, to give herself time to think. She'd listened back then, wishing he'd just be satisfied to stay in Texas.

John lifted her to the top of the ancient rock wall. Most of it had broken away and lay at their feet. They could still sit like they had when he'd spoken about seeing all the faraway countries…about leaving.

"Twelve years ago, I left without a real goodbye. I thought we'd broken up and didn't really see any sense trying to apologize. I admit to being cocky and that the idea of having a girlfriend back home wasn't my first priority. Dang it, I was eighteen." He laughed at his embarrassment. "I didn't think

I was coming back to Aubrey. For some reason, I never thought you'd leave."

"It's okay, I—"

"It's my turn, Alicia." He swallowed hard but didn't look away.

Whatever he had to say, it was important. Lauren was safe and John mattered to her. So she could hear him out before they went home.

"I was a hurt kid back then. I'm sorry. I've been around the world and back again, hon. And I know it'll seem odd, but I'm ready to come home. You can take as long as you need to 'get ready.' I'll be here when you are. I love you. I always have."

"My turn?"

He laughed and nodded, not releasing her hands.

"I sort of expected something like this when we pulled up. I mean, you said that you loved me back at the auction. Your actions, though—putting everything on the line for Lauren and me like you have… Well, you've shown me that you love me many times over in the past couple of days."

"I'm glad I was doing something right."

"I didn't want to feel like this. But not for the reasons you think. I kept thinking it would be disloyal to my marriage. Then Brian said he'd known his best friend and that Dwayne would be glad we were together. He's right. Dwayne would want me to be happy. He'd want us all to be happy. I am so ready to love you, John."

He tugged her to her feet and kissed her. The moment his lips touched hers, guilt-free desire took over. No more anxiety and no more questions. Being with him was her future. She was certain of it.

"Are you staying around here for a while?" If he wasn't, she had every intention of staying wherever he was stationed. "You don't have to give up your career in the navy, unless that's what you really want."

"I'm home for good. We should head back. You need to introduce me to Lauren."

"She's going to love having a dad."

HOME. IT WAS full, cramped, and John loved it. The house smelled like fried chicken, white gravy and peanut-butter cookies—his mom's recipe. Mabel had started cooking chicken nuggets as soon as Dev had pulled in the driveway with Lauren. Now the little girl, soon to be his daughter, was asleep in his arms and still had a chocolate-milk mustache.

She was a resilient kid and had voluntarily crawled into his lap. It might help that he looked exactly like Brian, who she'd known all her life, but today, he'd accept all the trust and love she shared.

"You're lucky I'm not fighting you to hold my

darling girl." Alicia kissed Lauren's forehead and then John's as she perched next to him on the chair.

"I thought I'd give you a break." He leaned his head back and was rewarded with a long kiss. Something he'd never tire of. He lowered his voice so only Alicia could hear. "Brian spoke to me while you were bathing Lauren. He's determined to find out who framed us and really set the fire."

"It was such a long time ago. Does it even matter anymore?"

"It does to him. He said he needs to clear our name, but it's more than that. I don't know what. I tried to convince him it didn't matter. There's time to sort it out later."

Alicia laced her fingers with his. "I can understand, but it seems futile. Maybe he'll feel different when things settle down."

"You two can stop your smooching, now. Right, Dad?" Brian lowered his voice as soon as he noticed Lauren. He set his cell on the coffee table before sitting in the only other chair in the living room. "This thing's been ringing nonstop. I didn't know anyone had my number. The sheriff said Patrick ranted about his ruined plans all the way to the hospital. It appears he was leaving for Mexico so he could kill Shauna, too. Now they're all headed for prison."

"Did I hear you talking about the mare earlier?"

"Yeah, with Dusty Phillips. You'd think he'd give us a couple of days before attempting to finalize the deal on the mare I've been trying to sell to him for weeks."

His dad tapped where his watch should have been. Seems he'd made a lot of improvements in the past two days.

"Why now?" Brian said aloud for him. "No auction of the Adamses' stock, for one. National championships for Carla. If she's riding again this year, she needs a new horse."

"Do you want to sell her, Brian?" Alicia asked from the arm of John's chair.

"No question of want. We have to sell her or lose this place."

"As soon as—"

"We aren't taking your money, Alicia," Brian said firmly, and his dad nodded.

Thank God J.W. was going to recover. He wanted the relationship with his father that Brian took for granted. He also wanted to restore the relationship with his brother. "How about mine?"

"We need a lot more than you've got in the bank."

Dev laughed from the kitchen, where he'd been helping Mabel with KP duty.

"There's ten grand in my room. How much do you need?"

"Where did you get so much cash?"

"He's really good at poker," Dev answered for him. "He also has no life. No rent. No real car. No women."

"I like my truck."

"Chicks hate it."

"That's true. But I figure I've got enough to get this place back on its feet, hire a couple of hands. Give Dad time to recover and give you a much deserved vacation."

"Johnny, I do believe you've shocked your brother into silence." Mabel dried her hands on her ever-present apron. "With that, you should all go find a place to sleep. Key to my house is under the third flowerpot on the back porch. I'm staying here in case your dad needs something."

His dad's expression was different than it had been three days ago. There was no panic in his eyes, just acceptance.

"I'm driving back to my cabin and inventorying my gear. If one cable is missing, I'm tracking it down." Dev held a finger in the air for emphasis, but destroyed his tough demand with a grin.

"I have a nice comfy bed in the other room. That means you guys can have Mabel's guest room all to yourselves." Brian laughed. "Good luck with your new family, bro."

"No luck needed when love's involved," John told him.

Alicia kissed his lips, stroked Lauren's cheek with a tender finger and rested her head on the top of his. "Piece of cake."

* * * * *

The TEXAS FAMILY RECKONING *miniseries
continues next month.
Look for THE RENEGADE RANCHER
by Angi Morgan
wherever Harlequin Intrigue books are sold!*

LARGER-PRINT BOOKS!

GET 2 FREE
LARGER-PRINT NOVELS
PLUS 2 FREE
MYSTERY GIFTS

Love Inspired®
SUSPENSE
RIVETING INSPIRATIONAL ROMANCE

Larger-print novels are now available...

ReaderService.com

Manage your account online!

- Review your order history
- Manage your payments
- Update your address

> ### *We've designed the Harlequin® Reader Service website just for you.*

Enjoy all the features!

- Reader excerpts from any series
- Respond to mailings and special monthly offers
- Discover new series available to you
- Browse the Bonus Bucks catalog
- Share your feedback

Visit us at:

ReaderService.com